Secre

Made in Savannah
Cozy Mystery Series Book 22

Hope Callaghan

hopecallaghan.com

Visit my website for new releases and special offers: hopecallaghan.com

CONTENTS

Cast of Characters

Carlita Garlucci-Taylor. The widow of a mafia "made" man, Carlita promised her husband on his deathbed to get their sons out of the "family" business, so she moves from New York to the historic city of Savannah, Georgia. But escaping the "family" isn't as easy as she hoped it would be, and trouble follows Carlita to her new home.

Mercedes Garlucci. Carlita's daughter and the first to move to Savannah with her mother. As a writer, Mercedes has a knack for finding mysteries and adventure and dragging her mother along for the ride.

Vincent Garlucci, Jr. Carlita's oldest son and a younger version of his father, Vinnie, is deeply entrenched in the "family" business and not interested in leaving New Jersey for the Deep South.

Tony Garlucci. Carlita's middle son and the second to follow his mother to Savannah. Tony is protective of both his mother and his sister, which is a good thing since the female Garluccis are always in some sort of predicament.

Paulie Garlucci. Carlita's youngest son. Mayor of the small town of Clifton Falls, New York, Paulie never joined the "family" business and is content to live his life with his wife and young children away from a life of crime. His wife, Gina, rules the family household with an iron fist.

Chapter 1

"You got any pasta still in the pot?" Carlita darted across the food truck, to the slow cooker filled with bubbling marinara sauce and thick, juicy meatballs.

"Yeah."

"I need two more spaghetti and meatballs." She waited for Mercedes to fill two to-go containers with pasta before adding the sauce and meat. She carried them to the counter and slid them toward the customer. "The total is twenty-one dollars."

The woman standing at the counter frowned. "I thought it included garlic bread."

"It does. Hang on." Carlita snatched two neatly packaged orders of garlic bread from the warming shelf and set them on top of the spaghetti. "Sorry about that."

"No problem. We tried to order half an hour ago and the line was so long we figured we would come back." The woman placed the exact amount of money on the counter. "By the way, I love Ravello's. Your restaurant has the best Italian food in Savannah."

"Thank you."

"The food truck is new," she said as she handed their order to the man standing next to her. "You weren't here during last year's Azalea Art Festival."

"This is our first time. It's going better than expected, considering we're already running out of some of our dishes."

"I'm glad we stopped by when we did. I would be heartbroken if I missed out on one of my favorites."

Carlita thanked them for their order and watched them walk away. "I guess we should've thought about adding a food truck a couple of years ago."

"We already got our hands full." Mercedes patted her mother's back. "And now you have Pete's restaurant and pirate ship on your plate. We're working almost seven days a week as it is. Don't get me wrong, the money is great, but I was thinking maybe you and Pete would want to slow down a little."

It was true. Carlita had more than enough to keep her busy. The newlyweds juggled thriving businesses—two restaurants, a pirate-themed tourist attraction, a pawn shop and rental properties.

Despite deciding it was time to coast into their golden years and enjoy the fruits of their labor, Pete and Carlita were busier than ever. Even before she came up with the bright idea to lease a food truck for the spring and summer season.

"I guess this is the price you pay for building successful businesses." Carlita winced, wiggling her aching feet. "I gotta swap out my shoes. These things are pinching my toes."

"I'll take over the orders." Mercedes slipped past her mother and waited for their next customer to approach the counter.

It was a twenty-something woman, tall and thin with intense blue eyes—the color of the Savannah skies in the springtime. Her hair, a beachy blond, fell to her shoulders in soft ringlets. The woman offered Mercedes a smile. "Hello."

"Hello."

"Is this the Ravello's food truck?"

"It is. At least it was the last time I checked," Mercedes joked. "What can I get for you?"

The woman ignored her question. "Are you an owner?"

"I...am. I'm Mercedes Garlucci."

"I figured as much." The beautiful blonde took a step back, tapping a blood red fingernail against her velvety red lipstick. "I'll take a tossed salad and a Romano's Italian Soda. Dressing on the side, please."

"Coming right up." Mercedes turned away to assemble the order. Her scalp tingled, and she could feel the woman watching her.

She abruptly spun back around, confirming her suspicions. The friendly smile was long gone, replaced by narrowed eyes. The woman's nostrils flared and Mercedes sensed anger oozing from her. An anger directed at Mercedes.

The woman flipped a switch. The enraged expression disappeared, replaced by a serene, almost sneering smile.

5

"Have we...have we met before?"

"No."

Mercedes bagged the food, added plastic cutlery and a couple of napkins before folding the top. "I'm curious. You asked for my name. When I told you, you commented you figured as much, which makes me wonder if we may have crossed paths before."

"We haven't. By design, I'm sure." The pretty woman pulled some crisp bills from her Brahmin crossbody bag and handed them to Mercedes. "Unless the name Natalie Lameron rings a bell. Perhaps we have a mutual friend?"

Mercedes repeated her name. "No. I've never heard your name before."

"Figures," the blonde muttered under her breath. She took her change and Mercedes thanked her, watching as the woman walked away. She didn't go far. In fact, she picked an empty seat on a small picnic table facing their food truck.

"What was that all about?"

Mercedes turned to find her mother standing by her side. "I have no idea. The woman knew who I was. She's pretty, but there's something about her. Maybe she's confusing me with someone else."

"She knew your name."

"The Garlucci family is famous." Mercedes brushed it off, making a joke about it, but every time she glanced toward the bench, the woman was there. Staring. Watching.

She finished her food. Tossed the wrappers in the trash and walked straight over to the Candy Cart, the sweet treat food truck parked nearby.

The blonde stood talking to the man at the counter for several long moments. It almost appeared like they were having some sort of heated discussion. Finally, she walked away.

"Hey, there." Elvira, Carlita's former neighbor, appeared at the counter. "You got any decent stuff left?"

"I don't know what you mean by decent stuff." Carlita rattled off the items still available. "I have a few slices of manicotti, chicken fettucine, breadsticks, salad and some minestrone soup. It's a good thing we're getting ready to call it a day."

"I'll take an order of manicotti and some soup." Elvira rested a light hand on the can of pepper spray clipped to her belt. "This has been one of the easiest gigs I've done in a while. How's biz been?"

"Going gangbusters." Carlita fixed the order and slid it toward her. "I'm not sure about keeping this pace for much longer."

"This is a long festival, good for the old pocketbook." Elvira patted her pocket. "How much do I owe you?"

"It's on the house," Carlita said.

"Thanks. I was gonna ask for a discount seeing how the food has been here for a while. Not that I mind leftovers."

"Leftovers?" Carlita gasped.

"You know what I mean. It's not as fresh anymore. Besides, I'm sure you're ready to get rid of it."

Mercedes patted her mother's arm. "I don't think she meant it as an insult."

"Elvira's mouth is as big as her heart."

"What's that supposed to mean?" Elvira's brows knitted.

"It means you're welcome." Carlita changed the subject. "Your uniform looks different. Is it new?"

"Yeah." Elvira straightened her collar. "I figured now that we're in the big leagues, I could afford to

9

spend a couple bucks and spiff up my company's uniforms."

Elvira Cobb, the owner of EC Investigative Services and EC Security Services, had snagged several big events in historic Savannah, Georgia. According to what she'd bragged to Carlita, the city was paying her security services company a pretty penny and had even negotiated a one year contract.

"It looks nice," Carlita said. "Very professional."

"Thanks. They weren't cheap. Luigi's cost even more. He's a big guy, so they charged me extra for his uniform." Elvira popped the container's top and dug into the food. "It's a good thing I have this sweet deal with the city. I was considering laying off some of my part-time employees."

"Your investigative services company isn't doing as well?" Mercedes asked.

"It's in the toilet." Elvira shoveled a large piece of pasta in her mouth. "I guess I'm going to have to invest a few bucks into advertising. You got any mafia stuff on the back burner I can tackle for you? Mob messes are always good for business."

Carlita placed her hands on her hips. "No. I don't have any mafia issues."

"What about theft? Any pawn shop or restaurant payroll discrepancies you need investigated?" she asked hopefully. "Surely, you have some sort of crisis in the works."

"No, and no. My books are balanced. My employees are great. Life is good."

Elvira polished off the pasta, tossed the empty container in the trash, and started in on the minestrone. "How's married life?"

"Great. I love Pete. Our penthouse apartment is beautiful. Mercedes is enjoying the extra space."

"You're living the dream. I gotta say, since you married and moved away, things are quiet. Too quiet. I'm used to Garlucci family action."

Carlita grinned. "In other words, you miss me."

"Yeah. It's not the same."

"I agree," Mercedes chimed in. "It's different without you around, Ma."

"I'm still around. Just not sleeping under the same roof." Carlita leaned her elbows on the counter. "This is a big festival. Maybe tomorrow I'll be able to take a break and check out some of the other food trucks."

"They got a little of everything. Pizza, hotdogs, a taco truck, Polish food. They even have a candy truck. It's called the Candy Cart."

Mercedes licked her lips. "Something sweet sounds yummy."

"Don't bother." Elvira polished off the soup and belched loudly. "Excuse me."

"What's wrong with the Candy Cart?"

"The food is terrible. I tried an elephant ear. It was gross." Elvira shook her head. "Maybe I got one from a bad batch cuz that place is one of the busiest food trucks here."

Ting. Carlita's timer went off, letting her know the festival had officially closed. "Let's call it a day."

"Speaking of calling it a day, I gotta check in with my staff." Elvira thanked her again for the food and hurried off.

"She's a trip," Carlita said.

"Elvira misses you. She's been over to my apartment borrowing sugar and salt. She even borrowed a roll of toilet paper and then she just hung around."

"Don't tell her I said this, but I kind of miss her too," Carlita confided. "She's like a nosy Aunt Rosey."

"I don't know about you, but I'm ready to hit the road."

Mother and daughter made quick work of storing the leftovers. They drove the food truck back to Walton Square, where Arnie, Ravello's restaurant manager, helped empty the leftovers.

"What time tomorrow will you be back to load up?"

"I was thinking seeing how it's Sunday and the festival doesn't start until eleven, maybe around ten."

"Sounds good. I'll have the food hot and ready to go."

"You're a doll." Carlita thanked him for helping and then limped out the back door. Mercedes was already there, staring at her phone. "Is everything all right?"

"It's Sam. I'm hosting a small party later. He said he'll be running late but won't say why."

Mercedes had confided in her mother some months back her boyfriend, Sam Ivey, who was also a tenant in her apartment building, seemed distracted and preoccupied. He'd even taken several trips out of town. Although the trips to visit friends appeared legit, Sam's distraction had been increasing. When questioned, he gave her various excuses...he was tired, stressed out, and busy.

Despite his insistence, Mercedes suspected something else was going on and even wondered if perhaps he was on the verge of ending their relationship.

"Maybe he's doing some special tour because of the festival."

"Could be. Oh, well." Mercedes shrugged and shoved her phone back into her pocket. "Tell Pete hi for me."

"Will do." Carlita gave her a gentle hug. "Thanks for your help."

"You're welcome." Mercedes trudged down the alley, and Carlita lingered, noting how her daughter's shoulders slumped. It was clear something was up with Sam. But what?

*****

Mercedes gathered up the trays of treats she'd assembled for the small gathering in the courtyard, proud of her charcuterie creations, which included a few of her favorite Italian treats.

She was finishing up when Autumn, her friend and neighbor across the hall, breezed into the apartment. "You should have called me to come over sooner. What can I do to help?"

"Grab some glasses and drinks."

It took a couple of trips for the women to carry the goodies down the stairs and to the gated courtyard out front. Mercedes turned the twinkling lights on and placed her Alexa in the corner, setting it to some soft background music.

Right on time, guests arrived, and soon, her party was in full swing, minus one person. Sam. Finally, she excused herself and stepped off to the side when she heard someone calling her name. It was her boyfriend, strolling toward her, his cheeks flushed and his hair mussed. "Sorry I'm late."

"What happened?"

"It was...something unexpected. It won't happen again."

"But..."

"I'm starving." Sam cut her off. "Your charcuterie board looks delicious."

"Thanks. I'm pretty proud of it myself."
Mercedes let his tardy arrival go. At least for now.
Until they were alone later. "You'll have to try the
prosciutto. I picked it up from Colby's Corner Store.
They just started stocking it."

The couple mixed and mingled, and Mercedes
started to relax. Sam was busy. She was busy.
Despite being distracted, he was still loving and
attentive when they were together.

Finally, the party wound down and guests
started to leave. Minutes past eleven, the last friend
had gone, leaving Mercedes, Sam, and Autumn.

"Let's have one more drink before we clean up."
Mercedes dragged a chair to the nearby table and
plopped down. "This was a blast. We need to host
parties more often."

Autumn lifted her glass. "A toast to the 'hostess
with the mostest,'" she quipped. "We don't make

use of this gorgeous outdoor space nearly as much as we should."

"It's definitely a lot nicer than it was when Ma and I moved down here." Mercedes thought back to the first time they'd seen the apartment building. It was old, basically abandoned, and in need of a laundry list of repairs.

There were times she wondered what had stopped them from hightailing it back to New York and selling the property as is. Her mother. Carlita had promised her husband on his deathbed to get their sons out of the "family."

With grit and determination, she'd done precisely what she set out to do, with the exception of Vinnie, her eldest son, who was "all in." As in—in deep. To her mother's credit, Carlita still hadn't given up and Mercedes knew she wouldn't until she'd taken her last breath.

Tink. A sharp echo coming from the gate caught Mercedes' ear. A flit of movement dashed past. "Someone is at the gate." She started to stand.

Sam sprang to his feet and stopped her. "Stay here. I'll see who it is."

Mercedes trailed behind her boyfriend, lingering several steps away. A shadowy figure moved under the streetlight. A very familiar figure.

Chapter 2

"It's her," Mercedes whispered under her breath.

"Her who?" Autumn slipped in behind her friend.

"A woman who ordered from our food truck today. She was acting weird." Mercedes explained how she'd asked if the food truck was Ravello's food truck and then wanted to know if she was Mercedes Garlucci. "It's almost like she stopped by to check me out."

"Obviously, Sam knows her."

"Yes. He does." Mercedes watched her boyfriend and the woman engage in what appeared to be a tense discussion. An inkling of suspicion inched up her back. Something told her—maybe it was women's intuition—this woman, Natalie something, was the reason behind Sam's odd behavior. Making plans to suddenly leave town and visit friends. Showing up late for dinner dates, tonight being a prime example.

"I'm going to find out what's going on." Determined to get to the bottom of who exactly this stranger was, Mercedes stormed across the courtyard.

"...my problem. You're behaving erratically and need help." Sam stood with his back to her.

Mercedes tapped him on the shoulder.

He abruptly spun around. "Mercedes, I told you I would..."

Fed up with all the secrecy, she quickly cut him off and addressed the woman. "Natalie, right?"

"Yes."

A flicker of surprise flitted across Sam's face. "You know each other?"

"Natalie showed up at the food truck today, asking questions."

Sam clenched his jaw. He spun back around. "Did you go to the Garlucci's food truck?"

A sly smile spread across Natalie's face. "I was hungry. And curious."

"Leave Mercedes alone," Sam gritted out, taking a menacing step toward her. "You've gone too far this time."

"Have I?" The woman shot Sam a triumphant look. It was clear she was taking pleasure in causing conflict. "Why did I have to introduce myself to your girlfriend?"

"You are no longer a part of my life." Frustrated, he ran his hand through his hair. "I can't believe I actually felt sorry for you."

Mercedes made a timeout with her hands. "Hold up. One of you needs to explain what is going on."

"Natalie is my ex-girlfriend," Sam said. "She tracked me down several months ago, asking for a loan."

"It wasn't a loan," Natalie argued. "Sam owed me money."

"That's debatable," he muttered under his breath. "Regardless, I gave Natalie money and thought I had seen the last of her. Until she came back into town needing more cash."

"Why would you give her money?" Mercedes' mind whirled. "An ex is an ex for a reason."

"It's complicated," he sighed. "She and I have a long and fractured history."

"Sam left me at the altar." Natalie proceeded to go into a lengthy explanation detailing their volatile relationship. "When he walked out on me, I fell apart and ended up in a mental institution."

Mercedes crossed her arms, pinning her boyfriend with a pointed stare. "You jilted Natalie. She went off the deep end. Now, she's back making you feel guilty, so you gave her some money."

Sam shifted uncomfortably. "In a roundabout way. I realized Natalie had other issues. Issues she kept hidden from me until it was almost too late."

Natalie's lower lip trembled. "I was heartbroken. Instead of working through our problems, Sam walked out on me."

"When your drug dealer showed up on my doorstep literally hours before we were to walk down the aisle." Sam sucked in a breath. "I recognize the look on your face. You're still doing drugs. You didn't need money to leave town."

Mercedes turned to Sam. "Why didn't you tell me? I would've understood, or at least tried to."

"It's much more complicated. Natalie won't take no for an answer. She isn't going to go away." Sam's expression grew pained. "She needs serious help to get off the drugs for good."

The woman placed a light hand on his arm. "Sam, darling. You're acting as if I'm not a part of this conversation. Please don't air our dirty laundry."

"There is no 'our' or 'us' and hasn't been for years. You need help. I'm not giving you another dime."

Natalie's lower lip trembled. "I need to pay Pooler tonight. If I don't, you might never see me again."

"We can only hope," Sam said. "It's the same story every time, Natalie. You're desperate. Your life is in danger. One sob story after another."

"I'm serious." Her eyes filled with tears. "Please. I need help."

Mercedes detected genuine desperation in the woman's voice. Perhaps her life *was* in danger. "How much money?"

"No, Mercedes." Sam adamantly shook his head. "I refuse to let you get pulled into this."

Natalie ignored him. "Fifteen hundred dollars. Cash."

"I don't have fifteen hundred in cash."

"What about jewelry, coins?" Natalie twined her fingers together. "You and your family own the pawn shop next door. I'm sure you have something of value Pooler would take."

"No way." Sam stepped between them. "Leave now. Before I call the police and have you arrested."

Natalie laughed. A harsh, bitter laugh. "Arrested? Don't be ridiculous. I'm standing on a public sidewalk."

He took a threatening step closer. "Leave and don't ever contact me or Mercedes again."

"And if I do?" she mocked. "What are you going to do?"

"Get another restraining order, one that won't expire this time," Sam said.

"Oh. I'm so scared," Natalie taunted. "A piece of paper has me shaking in my shoes."

"You are a disturbed woman, Natalie. It's not an attractive look," he said.

"I'm beautiful." The blonde tilted her head, her eyes glittering. "They don't pay ugly women to be runway models."

"You're a runway model?" Mercedes blinked rapidly.

"Was," Sam corrected. "Until her drug habit got in the way."

"I still am. I have an upcoming contract down in Miami next week."

"Good luck with that," Sam said. "Why don't you stay there while you're at it?"

"Jerk." Natalie swore, clawing at his arm with her fingernails.

He must've been expecting it, because Sam caught her wrist and shoved her away. "Don't ever try that again."

Mercedes stumbled back, staring at the woman. One minute, she was distraught. The next she was conniving, threatening, harassing and now she tried physically assaulting Sam. He was right. The woman didn't need money. She needed help. Serious help.

Something must have finally clicked. Natalie turned on her heel and began walking away. She mumbled under her breath, but she was too far away for Mercedes to hear what she'd said.

Sam stood stock-still until she disappeared around the corner of the building. He turned to face Mercedes, an unreadable expression on his face. "I'm sorry, Mercedes."

"You told me, years ago, about a woman you almost married. Natalie was the woman."

"She was. Natalie is a master at manipulating. There's something in her wiring, in her brain that trips. One minute she's thoughtful, sweet, kind. The next, she's conniving, cruel, and calculated."

"Bipolar maybe?" Mercedes asked.

"Who knows? She refuses to get help and relies on drugs to get by." Sam rubbed his brow. "I'm beginning to think I'll never get rid of her."

"You should get a restraining order," Mercedes said.

"I have. Natalie couldn't care less about a restraining order. You heard her. It's a joke, a worthless piece of paper. She's been picked up for drug possession. Jail time doesn't scare her."

Mercedes reached for Sam's hand. "We'll get through this."

He reluctantly pulled away. "I'm sorry, but until I can deal with Natalie once and for all, I think we should take a break."

Mercedes could feel the blood drain from her face. "Take a break? As in break up? Are you sure you don't have feelings for your ex? Because it's certainly looking that way."

"You don't understand. You don't know Natalie like I do."

She could feel a slow anger building. Sam had kept this piece of his past from her. A past which had shown up on his doorstep. Perhaps he still had feelings for the woman. Obviously, there was something to it if he'd given her money.

"Fine," she snapped. "Maybe you're right. Maybe it's time for you to sort through your feelings for her. Don't expect me to be waiting on the sidelines until you figure out which one of us you want."

"You have this all wrong." Sam grasped her arm.

Mercedes jerked away, her eyes flashing with anger. "Do I? You're right, Sam. It's time for a break."

Autumn must've caught the tail end of the conversation. She hurried over, an anxious expression on her face. "Hey, guys. At the risk of not minding my own business, I think maybe a little breather is in order."

"Mercedes..."

She turned her back on him. "Leave. Now."

Sam hesitated, looking as if he wanted to say something. He slowly turned and walked off.

Mercedes burst into tears as soon as he was gone. "What just happened?"

Autumn placed an arm around her shoulders. "I'm sorry, Mercedes. The woman is trouble. You and Sam need to take a step back and calm down. Once you have a chance to let the dust settle, I'm sure you can work things out."

"If not, Natalie wins." Mercedes sniffled loudly and swiped at her wet cheeks. "Who knows? She may have already won."

Chapter 3

The friends lingered, packing up the rest of the party's supplies before exiting the courtyard. While they worked, Mercedes half-expected Sam or Natalie to return. Neither did.

Back inside the building, Autumn offered to hang out and keep her company.

"I appreciate the offer. I think I'm going to call Ma to chat." Mercedes waited for Autumn to head to her apartment across the hall before stepping inside. She tapped out a text, asking Carlita if she was still awake and had time to talk.

Mercedes scooped Grayvie up and cuddled her cat close, wandering out onto the balcony overlooking the alley. Her phone chirped. Seconds later, it rang.

"Hey, Ma."

"Hey, Mercedes. Everything okay?"

"No." In one long breath, Mercedes blurted out what had happened. "The bottom line is Sam and I are taking a break. I'm not sure if it will be permanent."

"So you're thinking his unexpected trips out of town, running late for some of your planned dates involves Natalie, his ex?"

"It's looking that way." Mercedes paced. "Why couldn't he tell me what was going on? Why give her money or even the time of day?"

"He shoulda got a restraining order."

"He did. It expired. I suggested he get another one. Sam said it would be a waste of time. After what happened tonight, I have to agree. The woman is mentally unbalanced."

"Maybe Sam feels guilty. Like somehow he's responsible for her mental instability."

"Reading between the lines, I think he's trying to stay away from me because he's concerned about what this woman might do."

There was a long silence on the other end of the line. So long that Mercedes thought they'd been disconnected. "Are you there, Ma?"

"I'm here. Listen..." Carlita's voice grew muffled. "Let me throw some clothes on. I'm coming over."

"You don't have to. I'm an adult and can handle this on my own. I just needed someone to talk to."

"Yes. You're an adult, but I'm getting a bad feeling. This woman's actions scream instability. Who knows what she might try?"

"I have a gun. I know how to shoot."

"I know you do. Then let me come over to make myself feel better. Maybe I can run next door and chat with Sam."

"It might not be a bad idea. He loves you like a second mother."

35

"Give me half an hour, maybe a little longer. I have a key and will let myself in."

"Thanks, Ma." Mercedes, feeling slightly better at the thought her mother could, at the very least, offer some sound advice, ended the call, her eyes drawn to the building across the alley.

Her neighbor's kitchen light was on, and she could see someone walking past Elvira's window. Mercedes turned to head back inside. A small movement near the corner of the dumpster caught her eye.

A chill ran down Mercedes' spine when she saw it again. What if Natalie was still there...was in their alley watching her building?

She ran inside and grabbed a flashlight. Mercedes returned to the balcony, carefully beaming it along the front of the dumpster, searching for signs of the woman. She shifted the beam and ran it up and down Elvira's building.

"My eyes must be playing tricks on me."
Mercedes nudged Grayvie toward the balcony door.

Thud. She froze in her tracks, slowly turning
back around.

A defiant Natalie, her hands on her hips, now
stood in the center of the alley, staring up. The look
in her eye dared Mercedes to do something. A shiny
object caught the porch light. The woman was
holding a knife.

"Mercedes," she sing-songed. "Where's Sam?"

A sick feeling settled in the pit of Mercedes'
stomach. The woman sounded drunk, or maybe she
was high on drugs. "You're trespassing. I'm going to
call the police."

"I want to talk," Natalie said. "You need to
understand what Sam is really like. He has you
fooled."

"And you need help."

The woman became distracted, her gaze shifting to the pawn shop's rear window. She staggered across the alley. Mercedes watched in horror as Natalie began kicking at the window.

"I'm calling the cops!" Mercedes' hand trembled as she dialed 911.

"911. What is your emergency?"

"A crazy woman is trying to break into our pawn shop." Mercedes rattled off their address. "Please hurry. She has a knife."

Natalie stopped kicking and stumbled toward the fire escape which ran parallel to Mercedes' balcony.

She watched in disbelief as the half-crazed woman placed the knife between her teeth and began climbing the ladder.

If Natalie reached the ledge, she could easily shimmy across and hop onto her balcony.

"Sam!" Mercedes screamed Sam's name. She ran inside, slammed the door shut and did the first thing she could think of. She grabbed her handgun and ran back out, certain at any second the woman would be on her balcony.

Natalie dangled a few feet up in the air, chanting and panting. She fell to the ground and lost her footing. She staggered forward, under the streetlight, her eyes glazed over, as if she was in some sort of trance.

The knife was gone. Mercedes spotted it on the other side of the alley, near the recycling bin.

"I'm hurt!" Natalie screamed. "Help!"

Mercedes ran back inside and straight out of the apartment. "Sam!" She pounded on her boyfriend's door. No one answered. "Sam! Natalie is back!"

A shrill scream echoed from the alley.

Mercedes scrambled down the steps, taking them two at a time. She paused briefly at the landing, gripping the gun tightly. "Tony."

She dialed her brother's cell phone number.

"Hey, Mercedes."

"Tony, I'm in the alley. A crazy woman is trying to break into the pawn shop."

"What?"

"Hurry. I've already called the police."

"On my way." The call ended, and Mercedes hesitated.

She could hear Natalie screaming at the top of her lungs. "I'm hurt!"

Mercedes grabbed the doorknob. She hesitated. Was the woman hurt? What if Natalie was trying to lure her out of the house so she could attack her?

She sucked in a breath, tightened her grip on the gun, and cautiously eased the door open.

A wild-eyed Natalie stood mere steps away, holding the knife again. Her eyes widened at the sight of the gun. "You're going to shoot me."

Mercedes forced her voice to remain calm. "The police are coming. You need to stay away from here, from me."

"Where's Sam?" Natalie shrieked. "You shot Sam!"

"I did not."

"Sam's dead." Natalie raced to the end of the alley. She tripped and fell. Quickly recovering, she sprang to her feet.

Mercedes cautiously followed after her. "Are you okay?"

"Stay away! You killed Sam!"

"Sam is not dead." Mercedes struggled to keep her voice even. "You need help. The police are on their way. Let them take you somewhere."

"It's too late. He's after me. I don't have the money."

"Who is after you? You're not making any sense."

"This is all your fault!" Natalie shrieked loudly. "You took Sam from me and then you killed him!"

A loud *thunk* echoed from the murky darkness.

"He's here. I knew this was going to go down badly." Natalie ran away, disappearing into the dark night.

Mercedes pivoted, heading in the opposite direction, toward the safety of her apartment. She brushed up against the side of the building, ignoring the pain as her forearm scraped against the rough brick exterior.

She had almost reached the safety of her building when her neighbor's back door flew open. An armed Elvira appeared.

Tony emerged from his apartment above the restaurant and raced down the alley, gun in hand.

"What's going on?"

"Natalie. A crazy woman. She was just here and ran off," Mercedes said.

Tony started toward the end of the alley. Mercedes stopped him. "Don't go after her. She's completely off her rocker."

Woot. Woot. Bright strobe lights bounced off the wall. A police car sped down the alley, coming from the opposite direction Natalie had taken.

The doors flew open. Two officers appeared.

"The woman went that way," Mercedes said. "She tried busting out our pawn shop window and was climbing the fire escape."

"Hang on." One officer held up a hand. "I'll need to see some identification."

Elvira removed her wallet and flashed her driver's license. "Elvira Cobb, EC Investigative and Security Services. I can vouch for these folks. They're my neighbors and own this building, along with the pawn shop."

After checking her identification, things moved fast. A third officer arrived.

Mercedes gave them a brief description. The original responders split up, each going in opposite directions while the third officer stayed behind.

Carlita's car pulled into the alley. She sprang from the vehicle and ran toward them. "What happened?"

"Sam's ex was out here, trying to break into the pawn shop. Then she started climbing the fire escape. She's crazy," Mercedes said.

Elvira chimed in. "I heard someone screaming. At first I thought it was a feral cat and then I heard cursing. I saw Mercedes, so I ran out here to see if she was okay."

"Where is Sam?" Carlita asked.

"I don't know. I tried banging on his door, but he didn't answer."

Everyone began talking at once. Mercedes, Tony, Elvira, and Carlita.

"Start from the beginning, Mercedes," Carlita finally said. "What happened tonight?"

Mercedes filled them in from the moment Natalie arrived outside the courtyard. "I thought she was gone. After I called Ma, I went out on the balcony and noticed her over by the dumpster."

"The sight of you must've triggered her." Elvira tapped the side of her forehead. "She was wailing like a caged cat in a catfight."

"I called 911. Then, I called Tony. Natalie kept telling me she was hurt." Mercedes shifted her gun. "I tried to get her to leave, but it only seemed to make her even more agitated."

A familiar figure appeared at the end of the alley. It was Sam with his pup Sadie by his side. "What's going on?"

Mercedes crossed her arms. "Where have you been?"

"Sadie and I took a long walk."

"You missed all the excitement. Natalie was here," Mercedes said. "She tried busting out the pawn shop window and then she started climbing my fire escape."

"Seriously?" Sam looked around. "Where is she?"

"She ran off after I called the police."

Elvira picked up. "I heard someone yelling. By the time I got out here, the woman was gone."

Sam clenched his jaw. "I was hoping she wouldn't come back. I never thought Natalie would try busting out your window or climbing the fire escape."

"I think she's high," Mercedes said. "She was acting extremely unstable."

"Mercedes told me what was going on, so I thought I would come by to check on her," Carlita said. "Hopefully, the cops will find this woman and get her off the streets."

"And keep her from coming back here."
Mercedes briefly closed her eyes. "I've never seen anyone act so crazy. One minute, she seemed injured and needed help. The next she's screaming, calling me names, threatening me."

A pair of cop cars flew down the street, going right past them, and a sick feeling settled in the pit of Mercedes' stomach. She prayed the woman was okay and would get the help she desperately needed.

Tense moments passed. Ten. Fifteen. Twenty. At the half hour mark, Tony offered to track down the police. He made it as far as the end of the alley when one of the two responding officers reappeared.

Mercedes hurried toward him.

The cop aimed his gun at her. "Drop the weapon."

Mercedes dropped her gun. "Did you find the woman?"

"Yeah. She's dead."

Chapter 4

Mercedes blinked rapidly, struggling to process what the officer had said. "Natalie Lameron is dead."

"We found her not far from here." The officer consulted his notepad. "Is one of you Mercedes Garlucci?"

"I'm Mercedes Garlucci."

"The victim gave us your name right before she expired."

Mercedes started to sway. Sam reached out to steady her.

"I didn't hurt her. I didn't even touch her. She was here, trying to break into our pawn shop. I think she was on drugs. She said someone was after her and it was too late."

"She also said you shot Sam." The officer shifted his feet, motioning to his former colleague. "Was she talking about you, Sam?"

"Yes," Mercedes answered. "Natalie wasn't making any sense. She said I killed Sam and someone was after her."

Elvira cleared her throat. "You might not want to answer any more questions until you have an attorney present."

"Elvira is right," Carlita said.

The second responding officer returned. Soon the alley was swarming with cop cars and investigators.

Carlita pulled her daughter off to the side. "How are you holding up?"

"Okay." Mercedes placed a shaky hand on her forehead. "What a mess."

"This isn't looking good," she said in a low voice. "They're not saying how she died. Maybe she ran out in the street and got hit by a car."

"The woman was clearly agitated, maybe even on drugs." Mercedes shifted her gaze to Elvira's surveillance camera mounted in the corner and pointed downward. "Thank God for Elvira's cameras. They'll be able to show the police exactly what happened."

"Every moment you were out here with Natalie?" her mother asked.

"Except for maybe a few minutes, when I followed her to the end of the alley." Mercedes slipped past her mother, returning to the spot where Natalie had told her someone was after her, right before she ran off.

Carlita trailed behind. "This spot is out of range."

"It is." Mercedes leaned her head back. The realization that she and Natalie, near the end of their confrontation, had ended up in an area not covered by cameras was starting to sink in. "We were here."

"Did you still have the gun when you ran after her?"

"Yes. I mean, the woman was wacko."

Carlita drifted toward the pawn shop, noticing splinters of wood on the ground in front of the basement window. She removed her cell phone from her pocket and snapped a photo of the damage.

Mercedes trudged over. "This whole evening has been a nightmare."

Carlita glanced over her shoulder. "It looks like the cops are wrapping things up. They're probably gonna want you and Sam to go down to the police station and issue statements. I want to go with you."

"Why? There's nothing you can do."

"Regardless of what I can or cannot do, I'm not letting you go alone, even if Sam is there."

"Elvira is right. It looks like I'm going to need an attorney."

"Pete's got a good one. An old friend he trusts for all his business dealings. Let me make a quick call." Carlita stepped off to the side and phoned her husband, briefly explaining the situation. "The bottom line is the woman said Mercedes' name right before she died. The cops are gonna want to talk to her. I was thinking your friend, the attorney, might be able to send someone over to be with her during questioning."

"Buster Watson. He was at our wedding."

Carlita pressed her hand to her forehead. "I'm not sure I remember him."

"Perhaps not. There were so many people. I have his private cell phone number. I'll see if I can reach him." Pete told his wife to hold tight and he would call her right back.

Less than a minute later, her phone rang. "Buster is on standby. He said to send him a quick text and he'll meet you."

"Wonderful. I'll keep you posted when I know more." Carlita thanked him and started to end the call.

"Hang on," Pete said. "A word of warning. Buster is a bit...different."

"Different?"

"Flamboyant, eccentric, unusual. He's smart as a whip, but has a few quirks."

"Thanks for the heads up. The most important thing right now is having someone we can trust."

"I do. Implicitly." Pete reminded her to keep him in the loop before saying goodbye.

"Well?" Mercedes asked when the call ended.

Carlita waved her phone in the air. "We have an attorney on standby."

The women joined Tony and Sam. "Where are the cops?"

"Inside, taking a look at Elvira's surveillance camera recordings."

The minutes dragged by.

"This is taking forever." Tony lit a cigarette. "How long were you out here with the crazy lady?"

"Maybe ten minutes, tops," Mercedes said.

"Elvira has cameras on every corner. She's probably got several sets of recordings to show them."

"I'm going to see what's up." Sam and his pup entered Elvira's building.

Tony waited until he was gone. "I'm not the most observant guy on the planet, but I sense a chill between you and Sam."

"After Sam's ex showed up and caused a scene, he told me he thought we needed to take a break."

Tony made a choking sound. "His ex showed up. Sam dumped you. The ex comes back here, starts a fight with you in the alley and now she's dead?"

"It's not looking good for me, is it?" Mercedes slumped against the wall and closed her eyes. "They might as well throw the cuffs on."

"Not yet," Carlita said. "Think about it. She told the cops before she died that you shot Sam. Clearly, Natalie was delusional. So what if she said your name? She came here to pick a fight with you."

"She said something about it being too late and 'he,' whoever 'he' was, was after her," Tony reminded them.

"She must've been talking about her drug dealer." Mercedes jabbed a finger toward the splintered wood. "The woman was desperate. Maybe her dealer followed her here, waited until she left and then he killed her."

Carlita tapped her lower lip. "We need to find out how she died."

"Hey." Autumn hovered in the apartment doorway. "What's going on? Don't tell me Elvira tried blowing up her building again."

"No. Natalie showed up. She lured me into the alley. We got into an argument. She was acting all crazy, trying to break into the pawn shop, and then she ran off."

Autumn's eyes grew round as saucers. "Wow. So, you called the cops?"

"I called the cops, Tony, and Ma. By the time everyone got here, she was gone."

"I hope they catch the chick."

"She's dead," Mercedes said.

Autumn's jaw dropped. "Dead?"

"And my name was the last one on her lips before she died."

"How did she die?" Autumn asked.

"We don't know. Hopefully, it wasn't from a gunshot wound."

"You had your gun on you?"

"Yes. Because I was fearing for my life."

Autumn let out a low whistle. "I knew I should've hung out with you. Where's Sam?"

"Inside Elvira's place with the police."

"Her cameras," Autumn said. "Thank goodness for Elvira's cameras."

"Absolutely. Although I'm almost positive toward the end of our confrontation, we were out of range." Mercedes placed her head in her hands. "I wish I knew how she died."

"I can find out," Autumn said. "Where is she?"

Mercedes pointed her in the general direction.

"I'll go with you," Tony said. "Remember, there's a killer on the loose."

Carlita waited until her son and tenant hurried off. She turned to find Mercedes sitting on the stoop, a dazed look on her face. She eased in next to her. "This is a nightmare."

"It couldn't get much worse. Sam's completely unstable, drugged-up ex comes after me. I'm sure we're clearly on camera together. Next thing I know, she's dead."

Carlita blew air through thinned lips. "Remember, she also told the cops you shot Sam."

"A toxicology report will show what she was on." Mercedes shifted. "She seemed afraid. Afraid someone was going to take her out."

Carlita placed a light arm around her daughter's shoulders. "I know this is a lot to process, but try to think back. Do you remember seeing anyone else in the vicinity? Maybe at the end of the alley?"

Mercedes thought about it. She shook her head. "Actually, now that you mention it, I heard a *thunk*. Natalie must have heard it too, because she became even more agitated."

"So, maybe there really *was* someone after her." Carlita warily eyed their surroundings. "I don't like this. Not one bit."

"Me either. Elvira's cameras must've caught some stuff. The cops have been in there a long time."

Carlita consulted her watch. "I wonder how Tony and Autumn are doing. I'll give them a few more minutes."

Moments later, Autumn and Tony reappeared, trekking toward them.

"The cops are still inside Elvira's place?" Tony asked.

"Yeah. We haven't heard a peep," Mercedes said. "Were you able to find Natalie?"

"She's two blocks over. It looks like the coroner is wrapping things up," Autumn said. "One of my colleagues was on scene, reporting for the news station."

"Do you know how she died?" Mercedes held her breath.

"Yeah," Tony replied. "About that lawyer? Something tells me you're gonna need him."

Chapter 5

"Someone shot Natalie Lameron?" Mercedes whispered.

"Close," Autumn said. "They stabbed her with a knife."

"Her knife." Mercedes clutched her throat. "The one she had with her."

Carlita, hearing the panic in her daughter's voice, grasped her arm. "Natalie had her weapon. She left the area with it."

"But we were both out of sight." Mercedes held up her hands. "I'm clean. I don't have any defense wounds. No scratches."

"What happened to your arm?" Tony pointed to the fresh scrapes that were inches below Mercedes' right elbow.

"I ran into the side of the building, trying to get away from Natalie. I scraped it on the bricks."

Tony and his mother exchanged a quick glance.

"It's gonna be all right."

Mercedes swallowed hard. Motive and opportunity. She had both. And a weapon, not to mention injuries. Her stomach churned.

Before she could reply, a somber Sam, accompanied by both officers, exited Elvira's apartment.

She trailed after the men. "The camera angle was a little off. You can clearly see Ms. Garlucci was still on the premises when Ms. Lameron left."

"Momentarily," the cop corrected.

Mercedes hurried over. "Natalie left. You can see her leave, right?"

"She stepped out of the camera's range."

"It was all on Elvira's surveillance video. Natalie came here. She was flashing a knife. She tried

61

breaking into the pawn shop. I tried to calm her down, to get her to leave."

"I'm sorry, Mercedes." Sam lowered his head. "By all appearances, you ran after Natalie."

"Because she fell," Mercedes interrupted. "We were at the end of the alley. I was trying to tell her she needed help. Surely you saw us."

"We saw her run away. You chased after her. The next time you came into view was right before Tony and I showed up," Elvira said.

"I didn't stab her," Mercedes said.

The cop frowned. "How did you know she was stabbed?"

"Because we went over to find out what was going on," Tony said. "Autumn Winter, our tenant, and I told Mercedes how she died."

The officers excused themselves and gathered a few feet away. They began talking in low voices.

Carlita motioned to Sam. "Are they going to arrest Mercedes?"

"No, but they can ask her to go down to the station for questioning. My suggestion is to hire an attorney."

"We have one on standby," Carlita said. "It's a friend of Pete's. Buster Watson."

"Buster?" Sam arched a brow. "He's good. One of the best defense attorneys in the state."

"It sounds like we need the best."

An unmarked four-door sedan with tinted windows pulled into the alley. A man emerged and strode over to the officers.

"More cops?" Mercedes asked. "This guy looks familiar."

"Detective Polivich," Sam replied. "My guess is they'll want to question you now."

"I remember him. He investigated several crimes involving the Garlucci family," Carlita said.

"Which could be a good thing or a bad thing," Tony said.

"He's a hard nose," Elvira added. "We've gone around a few times. Polivich is strictly by the book."

"Question me right now? Here, or at the police station? They're going to arrest me and charge me with Natalie's death," Mercedes said in a flat voice.

"Not unless they have concrete evidence, although they might try to get a confession out of you or get you to slip up," Sam said.

Tony snapped his fingers. "It might be time to get the hotshot attorney Watson over here."

"I'm on it." Carlita promptly called Pete, who promised Watson was on his way.

"Do you want me to come over?"

"There's nothing you can do. I'll keep you posted. Thanks for getting someone over here so fast."

"You're welcome. I'm only a phone call away," Pete said.

Carlita promised she would keep him in the loop and ended the call, watching as Polivich finished speaking with the officers and made his way over. "Good evening Garlucci family."

"Hello, Detective Polivich," Carlita greeted him.

"I'll get right to it. Ms. Garlucci argued with a woman who was murdered this evening. Most of the confrontation was recorded by your neighbor. All of this means I have several questions for Mercedes Garlucci."

"And I'm more than willing to answer those as soon as my attorney gets here," Mercedes said. "He's on his way."

"An attorney already?" Polivich arched a brow. "Our investigation has barely begun."

"But it *has* begun," Carlita argued. "Considering you got right to the point, I'll be just as blunt. My daughter did not harm, touch, or injure Ms. Lameron. I'm sure when you view the surveillance footage, you'll clearly see the woman was unstable, not to mention harassing and stalking Mercedes, who promptly called 911."

"Are you speaking on your daughter's behalf?" the detective asked.

"I'm speaking in her defense. I wasn't here when Ms. Lameron showed up."

"Then I would ask you to keep your subjective opinion to yourself."

Carlita bit back a snarky reply. The last thing her daughter needed was for Polivich to have an axe to grind.

"Have you seen the surveillance footage?" Elvira asked. "I forwarded a copy to the cops. If you're interested in seeing it while you wait, I can access it on my office computer."

"I appreciate the offer Ms. …"

"Elvira. Elvira Cobb, owner of EC Investigative Services and EC Security Services. You may remember me. I have a partnership with the City of

Savannah, offering my security services for several public events."

"Actually, your name does sound familiar. Since you so generously offered to show me, I'll take you up on it." Polivich turned to a cop hovering nearby. "Let me know as soon as the attorney shows."

"Will do, sir."

Elvira and Polivich went inside. The cop returned to his car where the other officer stood waiting.

Bright beams of headlights bounced off the side of the building. A pickup truck coasted into the parking lot.

"It's Pete. Maybe the attorney is with him." Carlita ran to the end of the alley and caught up with her husband as soon as he emerged. "What are you doing here?"

"I couldn't sit at home, worrying and wondering. Your family is now mine. I'm as concerned about what happened as you are and thought maybe I could somehow help. Is Buster here?"

"Not yet. Detective Polivich is waiting for him."

"Wayne Polivich?" Pete asked.

"If his name rings a bell, he's worked on a few cases involving our family," Carlita said. "I'm not sure if it's a good thing or a bad thing. You know him?"

"Yeah. He has a reputation for being a ruthless detective who gets his guy, no matter what." Pete lowered his voice. "How is Mercedes holding up?"

"So far, so good. It's a mess. Sam's ex showed up right after her party ended. Apparently, the woman has been hanging around town, begging him to give her money. Remember when I mentioned Mercedes said Sam was acting weird?" Carlita didn't wait for him to reply. "Putting the pieces together, I think this woman somehow convinced Sam to help her."

"Or she was holding something over his head," Pete pointed out.

"Could be," she agreed. "Sam didn't want Mercedes to know. After she found out, he told her he wanted to take a break."

"Take a break?"

"From their relationship. Which is when Mercedes called me and I came over."

"By the time you got here, the ex showed up again."

"And started causing a scene," Carlita said. "Now, she's dead. One of the last things she said was Mercedes' name."

"Do you have any idea how she died?"

"Stabbing. Natalie had a knife. It appears she either stabbed herself or her killer used it on her. Although, based on how the cops are acting, I don't think the wounds were self-inflicted."

Pete grimaced. "I see Elvira is right in the thick of things. What about her surveillance footage?"

"I haven't seen it myself. I believe most of it corroborates what Mercedes said." Carlita told him near the end of the altercation, both women stepped out of the camera's range. "Natalie apparently owed her drug dealer money. She wanted money from Sam and then asked Mercedes for help."

"Where was Sam when all of this went down?"

"Walking Sadie," Carlita said. "I guess he needed some fresh air and was taking a walk."

"Hang on." Pete shoved his hands in his pockets. "Sam's ex is taunting, harassing and making aggressive moves against Mercedes."

"Including trying to climb the fire escape. She also tried busting out the pawn shop's basement window."

"Meanwhile, Sam is conveniently nowhere around."

Carlita's mind whirled. "Conveniently away. What if..." The thought was too disturbing for her to put into words.

"What if Sam ran into her after she left here?" Pete asked.

"Perhaps he took her out in self-defense." Carlita dismissed the idea. "Sam is not a killer."

"A former police officer? You never know what someone is capable of until they're thrown into a difficult situation."

"Hey."

Carlita turned to find her daughter-in-law, Shelby, hovering near the stairs leading to her and Tony's upstairs apartment. She darted toward them. "How's it going?"

"It's a mess," Carlita said. "Where's Violet?"

"In bed, sleeping. She zonked out about an hour ago."

"Thank God."

"Tony called to let me know what was going on. Are the police taking Mercedes down to the station for questioning?"

"No. We're waiting on Pete's friend, an attorney. Detective Polivich is here. He'll be questioning Mercedes."

"Polivich?" Shelby wrinkled her nose. "Why does his name sound familiar?"

"Remember the thugs who were targeting tourists? Reese had a run in with one of them when he was on her trolley. The guy ended up dead. Polivich investigated."

"You're right. I remember now."

"Do you need Tony?"

"No. I'm fine. I was just wondering how it was going."

"It might be a long night." Carlita gently patted Shelby's bulging tummy. "How's that growing grandbaby of mine doing?"

Shelby proudly patted her stomach. "Giving me fits. My latest craving is pork chops smothered in applesauce."

"It sounds yummy."

Shelby stifled a yawn. "I'm going to head back inside. I don't want Violet to wake up and wonder where we are."

"Tony will be home as soon as things settle down." Carlita gave her a warm hug and waited until she was gone. "Thank God the crazy woman didn't break into the apartments."

"Tony would not have let her get very far."

Ting. Pete's cell phone chimed. "Buster will be here in less than five minutes."

"Let's let the others know." Carlita slipped her arm through Pete's while they strode to the other end of the alley.

Elvira and Detective Polivich emerged.

"Well?" Carlita asked him. "I'm sure you can clearly see Ms. Lameron was the aggressor. She showed up here trying to get money, to cause trouble or problems for my daughter and family."

"I can't discuss an open investigation," the detective said. "I've already taken Ms. Cobb's statement and would like to get Mr. Garlucci's and Sam's statements while I wait. How much longer on your attorney?"

"He'll be here in a few minutes," Pete said.

"Taylor." A flicker of surprise crossed Polivich's face. "What are you doing here?"

"Mercedes is my daughter-in-law. I'm concerned about her welfare and want to make sure she's not getting railroaded."

The cop almost cracked a smile. "You make me sound like a jerk."

"Let's just say you have a reputation for being aggressive."

"I have a job to do and I intend to find out who murdered Ms. Lameron."

"I hope you do," Mercedes said. "Because as of right now, there's a killer on the loose."

A revving engine caught Carlita's ear. She shaded her eyes from the blinding headlights near the end of the alley.

"Here comes Buster." Pete, with his wife close by his side, went over to meet him.

The vehicle parked behind Pete's pickup. Several long seconds passed before the driver emerged.

Carlita blinked rapidly, certain her eyes were playing tricks on her. But they weren't. Buster Watson circled around the front of the vehicle and stepped under the streetlight. Her first thought was, *what in the world?*

Chapter 6

Carlita wasn't sure where to look first: At Attorney Watson's sky blue pinstriped polyester pants. The rainbow-patterned suspenders stretched over the top of his protruding stomach. His hot-pink collared shirt or his shiny black alligator shoes accessorized with what appeared to be yellow eyes and tail scales.

She said the first thing that popped into her head. "Are those alligator shoes?"

"Genuine Louisiana Cajun Bayou beauties," the man said proudly. "Of course, the eyes are marbles, but they look real, huh?"

Pete shook his friend's hand. "I see you haven't lost your sense of style," he teased. "I'm sure you remember my bride, Carlita, from our wedding a couple of months ago."

"Yes, sir. I sure do." Buster grasped Carlita's hand, shaking it so hard her head wobbled. "Old Pete lucked out marrying a beautiful Italian woman. I used to have a girlfriend who was from Naples. She was a real spitfire."

"We Italians have our moments," Carlita said. "Thank you for coming down here on such short notice, Mr. Watson."

"Buster. You can call me Buster. You're welcome. I see Detective Polivich is here. Has he started grilling and drilling yet?"

"No, but he's champing at the bit."

Taking turns, Carlita and Pete filled the attorney in on what they knew.

Carlita summed it up. "The bottom line is, Sam Ivey's ex showed up. He asked her to leave. She showed up here again and lured my daughter into the alley. The woman was acting erratically. Mercedes phoned 911. Before the police could get here and my son could make it downstairs, she ran off."

"And ended up dead," the attorney said.

"In a nutshell."

"Where was the ex-boyfriend when all this happened?"

"Walking his dog."

"You said your son and neighbor were in the vicinity," Buster prompted.

"Yes. But they didn't make it out here to help until after Natalie took off. As I mentioned, there's surveillance footage. From what we've been told, Mercedes and the woman stepped out of the camera's range for a few minutes."

"Giving ample time for your daughter to chase after her, force the victim to hand over her knife, stab her, and return home."

Carlita could feel the tips of her ears burn. "My daughter didn't kill this woman."

"Now hold up." Buster lifted his hands. "Don't get your feathers ruffled. I'm merely telling you what I believe the police are concluding. Your daughter had motive and opportunity. And a gun."

"Which wasn't the murder weapon," Carlita pointed out.

"And is beside the point. Stabbing her would be much quieter than pulling the trigger and having a loud gunshot echo in a quiet night."

"They can conclude all they want. Her fingerprints won't be on the murder weapon."

"Was your daughter injured in the altercation?" Buster asked.

"She scraped her arm on a brick wall trying to get away," Pete said.

"So, she sustained injuries."

"Correct," Carlita confirmed. "I'm sure she can tell you all of this."

"I like to get several versions, not just the version of the parties involved." Buster hooked his thumbs under his suspenders and rocked back on his heels. "I hate to say this, but I think your daughter will need legal representation."

"Which is why we called you," Pete said. "You're the best in the business."

"But I'm not cheap."

"We understand," Carlita said. "For now, I would like you to be with Mercedes during questioning."

"Let me have a word with her."

The trio approached the others. Pete made the introductions, and then Buster led Mercedes away.

Carlita warily watched from a distance. "What is he telling her?"

"He's going over what she should and shouldn't say," Sam said. "Watson's one of the best defense attorneys in Georgia. I'm sure Polivich is having a hissy fit."

"As long as he does his job, I don't care how much he charges." Carlita turned to Sam, pinning him with a hard stare. "I'm going to be blunt. This is all your fault."

"It is." Sam hung his head. "I feel terrible. I tried to deal with Natalie and keep Mercedes from becoming involved. Natalie was everything Mercedes said. Unstable, unbalanced, erratic, delusional, borderline schizophrenic. She needed help but never got it."

"Why didn't you come clean and tell Mercedes what was going on?"

"Because of Natalie. You don't understand what kind of person she was. Her goal was to destroy everything in her path, within striking distance. I was afraid she would destroy what Mercedes and I have...had."

"Despite your best efforts to protect Mercedes from your unstable ex, the exact opposite happened," Carlita said. "Look at where she is now? Having to defend herself."

Her pointed remark, squarely placing the blame on Sam's shoulders, had the desired effect. "I'll make things right. I promise."

Buster and Mercedes joined them. "Mercedes and I are ready to talk to Polivich and his team. This shouldn't take long."

Carlita made a move to follow them. Pete stopped her. "Buster works best when it's one on one. Mercedes is in the most competent hands possible. Let him handle it."

"You're right. It won't help having me hover." Carlita sucked in a breath, closely watching while Polivich pulled his notepad from his pocket and began writing.

Mercedes made several hand gestures toward the apartment, at Sam, at the end of the alley. All the while, the only thing Carlita could think of was none of this should have happened.

She felt a light tap on her shoulder and turned to find Elvira standing directly behind her. "While we're waiting, do you want to check out the surveillance camera recordings?"

"Yes. That's not a bad idea." Carlita and the others followed Elvira into her building, through her living quarters, and to her office in the front.

Elvira pulled up the first recording, the one showing Mercedes holding Grayvie. She stepped out onto the balcony, cell phone in hand.

"What time was this?" Carlita asked.

Elvira rattled off the time.

"This must've been when Mercedes was talking to me. It was after the party ended and Sam dumped her."

"I didn't dump her," Sam argued. "I merely told her we needed to take a break."

"Either way, Mercedes called me and I told her I was coming over."

Elvira hit the play button again and the group quietly watched as the scene unfolded. Natalie trying to break into the pawn shop. Her climbing the fire escape. Dropping the knife and then frantically searching for it.

The video ended.

Elvira accessed another recording, this one from a camera using a different angle. Mercedes followed the woman to the end of the alley and out of sight. Moments later, Elvira and Tony arrived.

"This is the end of the recording," Elvira said. "The cops show up, chase after Natalie, and find her."

"Can you forward copies to me?" Carlita asked. "I want to take a look at the video again when I have a clearer head."

"You got it." Elvira tapped the keys. "The cops already asked for a copy."

Tony stood nearby, staring at the screen.

"What is it, Son?"

"Natalie was after money or goods."

"To pay her drug dealer," Sam said. "She never came right out and said it, but I'm almost positive he was also her ex-boyfriend."

"She showed up at our food truck earlier today," Carlita said. "She asked Mercedes if she was the food truck's owner. When Mercedes told her she was, Natalie said something like she already knew it."

"So, she was researching the Garlucci family," Elvira said.

"I never mentioned Mercedes' name," Sam said. "Not even under my breath. Whatever Natalie discovered, she did it on her own. She specifically mentioned the pawn shop."

Carlita motioned to her son. "Do you remember seeing her?"

"I don't know. We get a lot of people passing through. Not to mention these images aren't crystal clear."

Elvira's office door flew open. Dernice and Luigi appeared. "What's going on?"

"Sam's ex showed up. She confronted Mercedes and ended up dead," Elvira said. "The cops are out back questioning her."

"Seriously?"

"I would avoid going back there until they're gone," Carlita advised.

"The cops and some big old tank of a car with bull's horns as a hood ornament is blocking the alley."

"Buster's car," Pete said. "I can ask him to move."

"Who is Buster?" Luigi asked.

"The attorney we hired to help Mercedes," Carlita said.

Dernice waved dismissively. "Don't mess with it. We can move the work van later. Is there anything we can do to help?"

"At this point, it's a waiting game." Carlita consulted her watch. "Hopefully, Polivich is wrapping up his questioning."

Heavy steps and low voices echoed from the back of the house. Attorney Watson and Mercedes appeared.

"Well?" Carlita asked. "How did it go?"

Buster cleared his throat. "We have some good news and some bad news."

Chapter 7

"Give us the good news first," Carlita said.

"Polivich took Mercedes' statement and seems to be satisfied," Attorney Watson said. "The police are packing up and should be out of the area in a few minutes."

"And the bad?" Tony asked.

"Although I'm not officially a suspect, based on the line of questioning, I'm also not off the hook." Mercedes turned to Sam. "You aren't off the hook either."

"And I don't have an alibi. Sadie and I took a walk, which may have been recorded on the pawn shop's front cameras."

"Detective Polivich plans to come back tomorrow to check out Savannah Swag's surveillance video."

"I'm surprised he didn't want to do it tonight," Dernice said.

"Polivich has his own way of doing things," Sam said. "He's methodical, in no rush, and has a solid track record."

"More than solid," Buster said. "My job for this evening is done. The longer I hang around, the more you're going to pay." He patted Mercedes' shoulder. "You have your marching orders, young lady. Mums the word. If the cops come a calling, you know what to say."

"I want my attorney present."

"You got it." Buster promised to check in with Mercedes the following day. Pete left to accompany him to his car and returned a short time later.

"This has been one long night." Mercedes briefly closed her eyes. "Correction. More like one long nightmare."

"I brought an overnight bag for you," Pete told his wife. "I figured you would want to stay with Mercedes this evening."

"I'm fine," Mercedes said. "I doubt Natalie's killer is after me."

"I can stay with her, Mrs. G. I mean Mrs. T," Autumn offered.

"Dernice and I will keep an ear out," Luigi said.

"I appreciate the offers, but I won't be able to sleep knowing all of this is going on," Carlita said.

"Let's meet up at Ravello's for breakfast in the morning, before we start work. We can go over everything we have," Mercedes suggested.

"I have some equipment we can use to take another look at the surveillance camera recordings, but on a larger scale. Eight works good for us," Elvira said. "We don't start our security shifts until nine."

With a plan in place, the group split up. Dernice and Luigi made their way to his efficiency apartment, with Autumn heading inside right after they left. Tony returned home. Pete was the last to leave, promising to be back in the morning for the meeting.

"I would like to have a word with Mercedes," Sam said when he, Carlita and Mercedes reached the upstairs hall.

"I'm only a holler away." Carlita slipped into her old apartment. Grayvie stood waiting at the door. She scooped him up, and he began purring loudly. "I bet you miss Rambo, huh? I'll have to bring him over for a visit soon."

She meandered through her former home, noting the changes Mercedes had made, adding her own personal touches.

Carlita checked the cat's food and water dish and noticed the dishwasher's panel was lit, signaling a clean load inside. Busying herself, she made quick work of emptying it and then wiped some breadcrumbs off the counter.

With a quick stop in the bathroom, she took a peek in Mercedes' bedroom, what had once been hers. It was neat and tidy. Everything in its place. Her daughter had turned the second bedroom into an office and painted the walls a pale shade of yellow.

She circled around and eased the front door open. Sam's door was shut. Carlita strained to hear voices, but it was quiet. Too quiet.

Restless, she stepped out onto the balcony overlooking the alley. By all appearances, the night was calm and serene, offering no hint of the chaotic scene only hours earlier.

Her gaze was drawn to Elvira's building. The place was loaded with cameras, capturing almost every angle of the alley, the street, the sidewalk, not to mention the Garlucci's apartment building.

Despite the extensive recordings, what the cameras hadn't captured was the final few moments of Natalie and Mercedes' confrontation. Had the woman's killer been lurking nearby, watching? Was it her drug dealer / possible ex-boyfriend?

Perhaps he had followed Natalie to Walton Square. Had been watching what transpired. Mercedes claimed the woman told her it was too late. "He" was after her. But then, she'd also insisted Mercedes had killed Sam.

Natalie's reality was blurred, distorted. Perhaps even upside down. Despite the troubled woman and her disturbing behavior, Sam had been wrong to keep his past relationship a secret from Mercedes.

Her daughter was a grown woman who could make her own decisions. If Carlita was in her shoes, she would have a hard time trusting him again, always wondering what else he was keeping from her.

"We might as well settle in." Carlita carried the cat to the couch and turned the television on, mindlessly flipping through the channels.

Another half an hour passed before Mercedes finally appeared. "You're still up?"

"Yeah. I'm gonna have a hard time sleeping tonight."

"Tell me about it." Mercedes flopped down in the chair. "What a mess."

"No kidding." Carlita set the remote on the couch, giving her daughter her full attention. "How did it go?"

"Sam apologized multiple times. He admits he was wrong and claims he was trying to keep me away from Natalie for my own safety."

"It backfired on him, big time. Are you back together?" Carlita asked.

"No. He asked me to forgive him, which I have." Mercedes told her mother he didn't want to pause their relationship and wanted to be by her side during the investigation.

"What did you tell him?"

"I needed time to think about it." Mercedes' eyes filled with tears. "It didn't have to go this way."

"No, it didn't. We all make mistakes. Having said that, this is his fault. I don't blame you for deciding you need some space to sort this all out." Carlita eased off the sofa and slipped her arms around her daughter, her heart breaking when she felt her body trembling. "I am so sorry. We're going to get through this."

"I'm exhausted. In shock. Hurt. Scared. What if the cops find some sort of bogus evidence and try to pin her death on me? I have no alibi, no proof it wasn't me." Mercedes showed her mother her scraped arm. "I can't even prove this was self-inflicted."

"I know it looks bad tonight." Carlita lifted her daughter's chin. Their eyes locked. "But you are a

Garlucci. We're a tough bunch. One thing I know about us is we stick together. There's no way you're going to be convicted of murder. Tomorrow morning, we're going to come up with a plan to track down whoever killed Natalie Lameron."

Chapter 8

"Where's Sam?" Carlita did a quick headcount of the people seated inside Ravello's dining room the following morning, taking note of a noticeably-absent Sam Ivey.

"I don't think he's going to show." Mercedes eased into the chair next to her mother.

"Let me guess. You did the dumping this time, and he's home pouting," Elvira said.

"Maybe."

"I don't want to badmouth Sam seeing how he isn't here to defend himself, but he made some poor decisions and now he's paying for them." Tony pointed to Elvira. "I see you remembered your projector screen so we can take another look at what went down last night."

"You got it. It's ready to roll." Elvira scurried over to the buffet table. "Everything looks delish. I'm starving."

"This is quite a spread." Pete lifted the lid on the chafing dish. A waft of steam burst out from the tray filled with fluffy scrambled eggs. He followed his wife along the line, adding slices of crispy bacon, sausage links, a petite ham and cheese omelet and topped it off with wheat toast slathered in butter.

"This all looks yummy, Ma," Mercedes said. "You musta got here early to prep for this kind of breakfast."

"I couldn't sleep," Carlita said. "All I could think about was how troubled Natalie Lameron was. She needed help and never got it."

"Not because Sam didn't try," Mercedes said. "In his defense, he practically begged her to get help."

"I know from experience you can only get help if you want it," Shelby said in a quiet voice.

"And thank God you did." Carlita lifted her plate. "You and Tony need to get over here and grab some food."

Elvira finished fiddling with the A/V equipment and grabbed her plate full of food. "I can't wait to dig in. Thanks for breakfast."

"You're welcome. Unfortunately, Mercedes and I are scheduled to work at the food truck again today, which means we don't have a lot of time." Carlita took a bite of her omelet and reached for her pen. "I figured the first step is to take some notes on what we know."

She jotted Natalie Lameron's name at the top of her notepad and began writing as the others rattled off what they knew about the woman.

-Drug addict.

-Sam's ex.

-Hanging around. Knew the Garlucci family's name and that they owned a pawn shop.

-Said it was too late. "He" was after her.

-Died from stab wounds. Not a gunshot.

"She was also hanging around the festival." Mercedes turned to Elvira. "You were working security yesterday. Do you remember seeing a tall, thin blonde with piercing blue eyes? She was pretty. As in runway-model pretty."

Elvira thought about it. "I have no idea. There were so many people there."

"The city has cameras in some of the squares," Dernice said.

"I'm sure the investigator will be all over it." Luigi shoveled a heaping spoonful of scrambled eggs into his mouth. "Did you tell the cops she showed up at your food truck?"

"Yes, and Detective Polivich seemed interested. He wanted to know around what time she was there," Mercedes said.

Carlita set her pen aside and reached for her fork. "We're off to a good start. Maybe we'll be able to add to our list once we check out the surveillance footage."

As soon as they finished eating, the busboys cleared the tables and Elvira dimmed the lights. The group grew quiet, watching Mercedes step out onto the balcony.

Natalie appeared and began behaving erratically, running back and forth, waving her arms in the air.

Carlita's breath caught in her throat when she noticed Natalie was holding a knife. "The way she's waving her knife around, I'm surprised she didn't hurt herself."

She lost her grip on the knife and appeared to stumble around, searching for it.

Mercedes emerged, gun in hand. Keeping her distance, it was clear she was trying to reason with the woman.

Somewhere along the way, Natalie found the knife and picked it back up. She ran toward the end of the alley. Mercedes cautiously crept toward her. Moments later, both were out of sight.

"What happened next?" Pete asked.

"She said it was too late and he was after her." Mercedes shivered involuntarily. "The timeline is a little fuzzy, but I think I remember hearing a *thunk* right after she said it."

"So someone could have been in the vicinity," Carlita said.

"Yeah. She got freaked out. That's when she ran off. Tony and Elvira showed up right after she ran away."

Carlita added the *thunk* Mercedes heard to the notes. "The takeaway is we need to figure out who 'he' is."

Ting. Mercedes' cell phone chimed. "It's Autumn. Natalie's murder is on the morning news."

"I figured it would air sooner rather than later." Carlita took the remote from Elvira, turned the television on, and flipped through the channels.

The room grew quiet once again as a breaking news banner popped up on the screen. A photo of the Garlucci family's alley appeared, followed by a front view of their pawn shop.

She turned the volume up. A reporter, one looking vaguely familiar, appeared. "...am standing in front of Savannah Swag pawn shop in Walton Square. Natalie Lameron, a former Savannah resident, was found stabbed to death in an alley not far from here late last evening. According to my sources, the investigators have several leads in the case and one of them is linked to this local business."

A photo of Natalie flashed across the screen.

"If you have any information about this woman, the Savannah police are asking you to contact them." A number appeared directly below Natalie's photo.

The news switched to local sports. Carlita turned the television off. "I'm all for free publicity, but not like this."

"I'm sure Polivich will make an appearance at the store today," Tony said. "The woman looks familiar."

"Chances are she was in the pawn shop snooping around," Mercedes said.

"As soon as I get over there, I'll check the surveillance recordings from the past couple of days."

"The sooner, the better," Carlita said. "The story is out, which means the investigators are going to want to solve the murder ASAP."

"It's not good for downtown business or tourism to have a killer on the loose," Luigi said. "Me 'n Dernice are working at the festival today."

"And me." Elvira jabbed her finger in Pete's direction. "I've been meaning to call you."

"Call me?"

"We have a deal. You promised me when you got back from your honeymoon that you and I were gonna team up to search for treasure."

"You're right. I did. Reluctantly. We have more pressing issues to handle. Namely, clearing Mercedes' name," Pete said.

"We'll figure it out. In the meantime, I was hoping you would, at the very least, give me access to your tunnels, the ones leading to the river, so I can take a look around."

Pete shot his wife a glance.

Carlita shrugged. "She's not going to let it go."

"Ever," Dernice said.

"Fine," Pete relented. "If you have time to stop by later this afternoon, I'll show you around."

"Sweet," Elvira whooped. "You won't be sorry. We're going to figure out where the treasure is. I can promise you that."

"Or die trying," Mercedes muttered.

Pete wagged his finger at Elvira. "You cannot bring explosives with you. In fact, I'll be doing a check before we go in."

"What about a single stick of dynamite, just in case?"

"No detonating materials. Period."

"Party pooper," Elvira grumbled. "If you insist. We'll go about it the hard way."

While Elvira badgered her husband, Carlita noticed Tony stepping in front of the blank television screen, a puzzled expression on his face.

She slipped in beside him. "What is it, Son?"

"I think I remember seeing the woman. She was a real looker. And I remember now, she was asking a bunch of questions."

"About the pawn shop?"

"About the pawn shop, how long we've owned it." Tony rubbed the stubble on his chin. "It's not unusual. People are always curious, but she seemed to have specific questions."

"I'm not surprised," Carlita said. "Obviously, she did her homework."

He nodded absentmindedly.

"There's something else," she guessed.

"Yeah. Something which might be significant."

Chapter 9

Carlita's heart skipped a beat. "You remember something important about Natalie Lameron when she showed up at the pawn shop?"

"Maybe. I don't want to get your hopes up, Ma. I'd rather not say anything until I know for sure," Tony said. "I'm gonna check the cameras as soon as I get a chance."

"And I'm sure the detective will show up sometime today."

"I would almost bet on it." He gave his mother a peck on the cheek. "I'm gonna walk Shelby back home and will let you know if I find anything."

"Thanks, Son."

The others trickled out. Elvira, Luigi, and Dernice, who said they would see Carlita and Mercedes at the festival later.

Mercedes ran home to change, leaving Carlita and Pete behind.

"Well?" Pete placed his arms around his wife and pulled her close. "Is my super sleuth wife going to figure this one out?"

"It's not a matter of if, but when." Carlita straightened his shirt collar. "Based on Mercedes' recollection and what the woman said, it's clear the drug dealer / ex-boyfriend is behind her death."

"You're going to have your work cut out for you, figuring out who he is."

"I wish Sam would've made an appearance. He might have been able to shed some light on who this guy is."

"The police already questioned him," Pete said. "I'm sure he told them what he knew."

"I hope the cops aren't giving him preferential treatment, asking him a few standard questions and then giving him a pass."

"You're upset," Pete said.

"More like aggravated. It didn't have to happen this way. Sam should have told Mercedes what was going on. When you're a couple, you expect honesty and trust."

"Meaning you wonder about his level of commitment if his ex was hanging around and he was keeping it a secret?"

"Exactly. If Sam kept this from Mercedes, what else is he keeping from her?" Carlita asked.

"Which is probably why she decided a break was the way to go. Mercedes is smart. She's beautiful, caring, loyal," Pete said. "She's wisely stepping back and reassessing their relationship. You mentioned he'd been acting a little evasive and distracted for a while now."

"He has and something tells me it had everything to do with Natalie Lameron. Maybe there's more to the story about his previous relationship."

"It could be." Pete placed a light kiss on his wife's forehead. "She knows her family has her back. We'll be right here for her, no matter what."

"Exactly. Our number one priority is to clear Mercedes' name. What she and Sam decide to do going forward is entirely up to them. Either way, I support her decision."

"As do I."

After Pete left, Carlita headed to the kitchen to help load the food truck. Mercedes showed up a few minutes later, and they made quick work of gathering the supplies they would need for another busy day.

The sun was high in the sky by the time they arrived at their designated spot, the same one they'd had the previous day and would keep for the duration of the festival.

Mother and daughter set up. They lifted the rolling window moments before their first customer arrived.

Business was brisk. They dished out pasta, stuffed rolls of manicotti, homemade spaghetti and thick juicy meatballs, creamy parmesan chicken, crisp salads, fresh breadsticks, and hearty bowls of minestrone.

The hours flew by. Soft jazz mingled with a chorus of trombones drifting from a small stage not far from Freedom Square's fountain set the mood. Bright beams of sunlight filtered through the majestic oaks shading their spot.

Carlita could almost smell the gardenias. "I love spring." She closed her eyes and breathed deeply. "There's nothing like Savannah in the springtime."

"It's wonderful," Mercedes said. "The gardenias are my favorite. Along with the azaleas and camellias."

Carlita filled another to-go box and counted out the customer's change. She thanked them for the business and gave her daughter a side glance, noting the somber expression on her face. "You okay?"

"I'm a little stressed out."

"And understandably so. Have you heard from Sam?"

"He sent a text earlier, asking how I was doing and telling me he was sorry for the umpteenth time." Mercedes leaned her hip against the cooler. "What do you think?"

"I've already shared my thoughts. Sam was wrong. There should be a certain level of honesty in a relationship. He failed on his end by not telling you what was going on...for months."

"I agree. He said..." Mercedes' voice faded.

"Said what?" her mother prompted.

"He knew Natalie was deeply disturbed. He was trying to handle it, to convince her to go away without involving me."

"It backfired. Big time."

"He realizes it now. Regardless, hindsight is 20 / 20. Coulda, shoulda, woulda."

"Tony told me he might have something. He thinks he remembers Natalie coming into the pawn shop."

Mercedes brightened. "Something to help us figure out who killed her?"

"Yeah. He didn't want to get our hopes up. He said he would let me know. I figured I would run by there later, after we finish our shift."

"I heard Elvira badgering Pete about checking out his tunnels."

"He told her she could swing by the restaurant this afternoon and have a look around. I plan to be there to keep her in line." Carlita glanced over her daughter's shoulder. "Speaking of the devil. Here she comes now."

Elvira casually strolled over. "Hey, Carlita."

"Hello, Elvira." Carlita leaned her elbows on the counter. "Let me guess. You're hungry."

"No way. I'm still full from breakfast." Elvira tapped the top of her watch. "I was thinking about heading over to Pete's around half past three."

"Half past three works for me. I'll meet you there."

"Why? You have an interest in treasure, after all?"

"No. My interest is in keeping an eye on you," Carlita joked.

"I already promised Pete I wouldn't bring explosives. Although, I will bring the map I found, have a look around, maybe snap a few pictures."

Carlita arched a brow. "You have no plans to excavate, dig, sift, hammer?"

She shrugged, refusing to meet Carlita's gaze. "I mean, I might bring a few smaller tools."

"That's what I thought."

Mercedes leaned in. "I like your bracelet. Where did you get it?"

Elvira lifted her wrist, showing off her bracelet with a silver circle. "From my beau, Sharky. It's a charm bracelet. Check it out." She slid the bracelet from her wrist and set it on the counter before carefully lifting the lid.

Inside were several small charms—a ship, an anchor, a Siren of the Seas' logo, a seahorse and a turquoise gemstone.

"The bracelet is adorable," Mercedes said. "How thoughtful. It's very well made."

"Sharky wouldn't tell me how much he paid for it. All he said was I was worth every penny."

"He's a special man," Carlita said. "It's a nice gift."

"Thanks. He's going to Alaska."

"Going to Alaska?" Mercedes echoed.

"Siren of the Seas is spending the summer in Alaska."

"It's going to be hard for you two to sneak away during his breaks," Carlita said.

Elvira waved dismissively. "It'll be fine. He'll be back in Florida before I know it. Who knows? Maybe I'll hop on a plane, fly over and surprise him."

"You mean show up on the ship without telling him you're coming?"

"Yeah." Elvira's eyes lit. "I kinda like the idea. He would be geeked."

"Or freaked," Mercedes joked. "Have you ever been to Alaska?"

"Once. It was a long time ago." Elvira shifted her gaze. "I don't get it."

"Don't get what?"

"How busy the Candy Cart is. I bought an elephant ear there yesterday. It was gross. It tasted like old oil. I could barely chew it."

"Something sweet sounds good." Mercedes untied her apron. "Do you mind if I run over and grab something?"

"Go ahead." Carlita watched as Mercedes exited the food truck and hustled across the grass.

"How's she holding up?" Elvira asked after she was out of earshot.

Carlita tipped her hand back and forth. "Obviously, she's hurt. Sam messed up. It's going to take some time for Mercedes to trust him again."

"Messed up big time. I hate to state the obvious, but I'm sure the cops will focus on her."

"I agree, which is why we need to figure out who killed Natalie."

Mercedes returned, ending their conversation. "I bought an order of fried peach pies. We can all try one." She handed one to Elvira and another to her mother.

"They look okay." Mercedes dipped it in the cup of sugar glaze that came with it and took a big bite. She promptly spit it out. "Yuck."

Elvira ran to the trash and spit hers out.

Carlita hadn't yet taken a bite of the peach pie. "What's wrong?"

"It's awful." Mercedes grimaced. "It tastes like sardines."

Carlita tentatively took a sniff. "It smells like rancid oil. I don't get it. They're the busiest food truck around, yet their food is awful."

Elvira tossed the rest of her pie in the trash. "Maybe their main selling item isn't sweets."

"It's clearly a sweet treats truck," Carlita said.

"Do you know what candy cart is slang for?"

"No."

"Drugs," Elvira said.

Mercedes made a choking sound. "This is all...beginning to make perfect sense."

Chapter 10

"What's starting to make perfect sense?" Carlita asked.

"Natalie ordered food from us and then she went to the Candy Cart. I forgot all about it until now," Mercedes said. "Or maybe it was me not understanding the significance. What if the Candy Cart is a front for drugs?"

"I wouldn't be surprised considering the garbage they're trying to pass off as edible goods," Elvira said. "Three or four of the same people have been working both days. I could go order food and see what's up."

"You mean sort of scope them out?" Mercedes asked.

"Exactly." Elvira held out her hand.

"What?"

"I'm doing this as a favor for you. I need cash to order something."

"Good grief." Carlita snatched a ten-dollar bill from the cash drawer and handed it to her. "Try to find edible food this time."

"Something tells me that is gonna be nearly impossible." Elvira tucked the bill in her pocket and sauntered off.

Mother and daughter watched her wait in line. She placed her order and began fumbling around.

"Great. I think she misplaced the money," Mercedes muttered.

"No. I think she's stalling, buying time."

Elvira finally handed the guy the money. She did a fast turn and tripped on a cord. The plate flew from her hand and she fell to her knees.

The food truck door blew open. Two workers ran to Elvira's aid. She slowly rose to her feet, swiped at her pant leg, and pointed to the plate of food now upside down in the grass.

A worker helped her to the bench while another ran back inside the food truck. The woman returned moments later, holding a new dish.

Meanwhile, another worker, an older man in his late forties or early fifties, exited the back. He moved the cord Elvira had tripped on before making his way over to her.

"He's the boss," Carlita murmured. "I wonder if he's the owner."

"I was wondering the same thing."

Finally, the workers and the man who appeared to be in charge returned to the truck. Elvira made several funny faces as she nibbled the food. She finally tossed most of it in the trash before heading in the opposite direction.

"She's gone," Carlita said after she walked out of sight. "What a waste of ten bucks."

Knock. Knock.

Mercedes darted to the door. She eased it open and found Elvira standing on the other side. "What are you doing?"

"Keeping a low profile. It's surveillance 101. I didn't want the Candy Cart people to see me go right from their food truck to here."

"Ah. In case there's a connection between them and Natalie Lameron." Mercedes ushered her inside. "Good idea. What did you find out?"

"The older, slightly balding guy appears to be the owner or manager. The other two doofuses had no clue what was going on."

"Did you trip, or was it on purpose?" Carlita asked.

"I saw the cord, started to step around it and changed my mind." Elvira winced. "I should have fallen the other way. Instead, I landed on my bad knee."

"I'm sorry you got hurt," Carlita apologized. "How was the food?"

Elvira gave them a thumbs down. "I figured the fried foods would be bad, so I tried a piece of mint chocolate chip fudge and some slices of chocolate-covered bacon." She made a barfing sound.

"I take it the fudge and bacon weren't edible."

"Not even close. They're obviously not luring customers in with their culinary creations." Elvira wiped her mouth with the back of her hand. "It's definitely time to take a closer look at Candy Kanye."

"You got his name?" Carlita clapped her hands. "Way to go."

"Don't break out the party balloons yet. I made the nickname up. Although it shouldn't be hard to get the 4-1-1 on the Candy Cart," Elvira said. "Seeing how EC Security Services is in charge of security, I have the roster, a list of the companies who are here."

"Why didn't you mention this earlier?" Mercedes asked.

"Because I didn't know there was a potential connection between the deceased and Candy Kanye." Elvira belched loudly. "Excuse me. The disgusting food is upsetting my delicate digestive system."

"Anyone who can eat natto has a stomach of steel," Carlita said.

"It's the grease. Me and grease don't mix well." Elvira glanced over her shoulder. "I need to get back to my beat. We'll catch up later over at Pete's. I should have some new info on the Candy Cart by then."

Carlita thanked her and closed the door after she left. A group of customers approached, which meant it was back to business for the rest of their shift.

At three on the dot, Ravello's manager and a kitchen worker arrived to take over.

On their way out, Carlita and Mercedes strolled around Freedom Square, passing by the Candy Cart.

"The more I think about it, the more I believe the Candy Cart is a cover for something else," Mercedes said. "Natalie was talking to the workers for a reason."

"Just like she stopped by our food truck for a reason," Carlita said. "We have a few more minutes before I meet up with Pete and Elvira. I figured we could swing by the pawn shop to check in with Tony."

Sunday afternoon meant the shop was busy, but not so much that Carlita and Mercedes had to hang around and wait for Tony.

"Hey, Ma. Mercedes. How's the food truck biz?"

"Busy. The next couple of days should be slightly slower, seeing how the weekend is over. On the other hand, it's spring break, which means a lot of vacationers are in town, so maybe we'll still draw big crowds." Carlita changed the subject. "Have you checked out the surveillance to see if you caught Natalie on camera?"

"I did, and we did."

"Have her on video surveillance," Carlita confirmed.

"Yeah. Remember when I mentioned I might have something?" Tony didn't wait for her to answer. "I was right."

Mercedes clapped her hands. "What is it?"

"Before we go there, Detective Polivich stopped by. I showed him the surveillance footage. We both agreed Natalie Lameron was definitely scoping the place out."

"To break in and steal stuff?" Mercedes asked. "If that was her plan, why bother drawing attention to herself?"

Carlita twirled a finger against her forehead. "Remember, the woman had some mental and drug issues. I'm sure she wasn't thinking clearly."

"Polivich asked some questions, about Sam and Mercedes, how I would describe their relationship."

"It's non-existent," Mercedes said. "At least for now."

"What did you tell him?" Carlita asked.

"I told him it was none of my business. If he needed to know the status, he needed to go to the source."

"Thanks, Son."

Tony led them to the counter in the back. "I also got this from Attorney Buster Watson." He handed his mother a sheet of paper. She burst out laughing.

"What's so funny?" Mercedes leaned in, her eyes drawn to the top of the sheet where a "larger than life" glamor shot of the attorney was prominently displayed. "What is he wearing?"

"My guess is Hugh Hefner's velvet smoking robe." Tony chuckled. "He's even got the pipe."

Sure enough, Buster sported a deep red velvet jacket with black lapels. Perched atop his plump head was a captain's hat. He held a hand-carved wood pipe with tendrils of smoke curling out of the top.

A busty brunette with a sultry expression on her face hovered in the background. "Is this his...girlfriend?" Mercedes' eyes grew round as saucers.

"I have no idea. The picture is a little tacky but who am I to judge? To each his own." Carlita skimmed the bill, her breath catching in her throat when she got to the bottom, and noticed the "amount due."

"Three hundred dollars an hour," she gasped. "We already owe him four hundred bucks."

"Someone has to pay for all that sexy loungewear," Tony joked. "The charges seem a little steep."

Carlita folded the bill in thirds and tucked it in her pocket. "I had hoped because he and Pete are friends, he would give us a friend and family discount."

"If this is the friends and family discount, I would hate to see what his regular hourly rate is," Mercedes said. "I'm sorry, Ma. You can take it out of my paycheck."

"No way." Carlita shook her head. "If Buster's expertise keeps you from spending even one minute locked up, it was well worth the cost."

"Absolutely. I want to show you what I found on the surveillance cameras." Tony tapped the keyboard. He pulled up the link to the monitoring system. "This was right before we closed last night."

The pawn shop's front door opened. Natalie stepped inside and lingered in the doorway. She shot a glance over her shoulder before slowly making her way up and down the aisles.

She approached the gun case and paused momentarily before moving on to the jewelry display case. Natalie spent a long time perusing the inventory.

Tony approached and said something to her. She shook her head.

"I was asking her if she needed help."

He turned to go and walked several steps away. Not too far, but far enough to give her space.

"You're keeping an eye on her," Carlita said.

"Yeah. I was gettin' the vibe something was up," Tony said. "In this business, you always gotta go with your gut, especially near closing when most thugs decide it's the best time to rob you."

"Because we have more money on hand," Carlita said.

"Bingo."

The recording continued. Another pawn shop employee approached Natalie. Once again, she shook her head.

Tony circled around the perimeter of the pawn shop. He lingered briefly near the doors before walking down the center aisle.

Natalie left two minutes later.

"So she scoped the place out and left," Mercedes said.

"You're missing it," Tony said.

"Missing what?"

"This." He slid the recording bar back and hit play. Once again, Natalie entered the shop and made her rounds. "Do you see it now?"

"No." Mercedes shook her head.

Carlita squinted her eyes and stared at the screen. "I do. Will you look at that?"

Chapter 11

"I'm obviously not seeing something," Mercedes said. "All I see is Natalie scoping out our pawn shop and leaving."

"This." Carlita touched the screen. "Outside the door."

"It's a guy smoking a cigarette. Which isn't uncommon considering smoking isn't allowed inside."

"It's not the fact he's outside and smoking," Tony said. "If you pay attention, he showed up at almost the exact same time as Natalie. Check this out. Check out what happens next."

Carlita's breath caught in her throat as she watched the man wearing a knitted cap enter the store shortly after Natalie did.

She nervously glanced in his direction, and then quickly turned away.

Meanwhile, the man sauntered over to the gun case. Tony appears and shows the man a handgun. They chat for a few minutes. She leaves. He leaves.

"You're right," Mercedes said. "They must have been together."

"I was thinking the same thing."

"Did you point this out to Detective Polivich?" Carlita asked.

"Yes. I set the gun aside to make sure we didn't end up with other prints on it. While Polivich was here, he dusted it."

"For prints," Carlita said. "Maybe they'll get a match and have someone else they can question."

"Unless the guy doesn't have a record," Tony pointed out.

"True. Can you zoom in on him?" Mercedes asked.

"Yeah. I've looked at it several times. You can't see the guy's face. He's clearly aware of the cameras and is avoiding them."

"But you got a good look at him," Carlita said.

"Not really." Tony shrugged. "So many people come in and out of here every day. I gave Polivich a description, but he could've been anybody on the street. Notice the cheesy mustache?"

Carlita's eyes squinted. "Yeah."

"A hundred bucks says it's fake. What about the cameras outside the building?" Mercedes asked.

"Again, there's no clear shot of his face. It's almost like the guy knew there were cameras."

Carlita pressed her palms together. "Something tells me Natalie is linked to the Candy Cart."

"What's the candy cart?" Tony asked.

"It's a food truck," Mercedes explained. "Natalie stopped by our food truck and then I remember her going over there. She was talking to the workers. I think she knew them."

"Maybe she was trying to score some free food," he said.

"The food is disgusting. As in inedible. Even Elvira agreed."

"You think Natalie was buying drugs from the food truck?"

"Maybe. Elvira seems to think the Candy Cart is slang for a drug dealer." Carlita tapped the top of her watch. "Speaking of which, I need to get going. She's probably already over at Pete's place sitting on his doorstep, itching to get into his tunnels."

"I'll let you know if I come up with anything else," Tony promised.

Mercedes and her mother exited through the back and stepped into the hall.

"Do you want me to spend tonight with you?" Carlita asked.

"Nah." Mercedes waved dismissively. "I'll be fine. If the drug dealer took Natalie out, he's not after me."

"Unless he thinks you may have seen him," her mother said.

"True. I feel safe. Sam is here. Autumn, Luigi, Cool Bones. Plus, I have my gun."

Carlita gave her a gentle hug. "I don't want to be a hovering mother. I'm only a phone call away. Are you covering a shift at Ravello's?"

"Yeah. I have an hour or so before I go in. I'm thinking about whipping up a chocolate chip peanut butter pie, something that's edible. In fact, after I'm done, I might sit down and eat the entire thing myself."

"It sounds delicious. I can't envision you eating an entire pie, no matter how upset you are. Save a piece for me." Carlita left, but not before reminding her daughter to call if she needed her.

After she was gone, Mercedes tracked down the recipe she'd saved on her computer. Peanut butter was one of Sam's favorites. It was also one of hers.

She began gathering the ingredients and assembled the pie crust first. After finishing, Mercedes grabbed a hand mixer and whipped the heavy cream. She set it aside and worked on beating the cream cheese.

"This looks smooth enough." Humming under her breath, she added sugar, peanut butter, and vanilla. Finally, it was time to add the heavy whipped cream and dark chocolate chips.

She blended the filling and filled the pie crust before popping it into the freezer. "This looks yummy—much better than the yucky deep fried peach pies."

Mercedes checked the clock. It was time to get ready for work. She briefly wondered how her mother was faring with Elvira and her relentless quest for riches.

One thing was certain. Her mother had her hands full.

*****

Elvira slid the headlamp on top of her head and adjusted the lens. She rummaged around inside her backpack and handed Carlita a heavy-duty flashlight. "You can use this."

"For what?"

"To keep an eye peeled for clues."

"I think you're setting your expectations too high," Pete warned. "I've been through these tunnels dozens of times. Maybe even hundreds."

"But not with this baby." Elvira waved her phone in the air. "I snapped a photo of the map I found on the wall. Would you like me to send you a copy?"

"And part with valuable information?" Carlita playfully pressed a hand against Elvira's forehead. "Are you feeling all right?"

She swatted it away. "We're getting down to the nitty-gritty. I figured, seeing how Pete and I are partners, we need to share what we have."

"I thought you were hot on the trail of treasure buried at sea," Carlita said.

"Sharky and I did some preliminary research. So far, I haven't found anything but who knows? Maybe there are multiple treasures waiting to be found." Elvira tapped the top of her phone. "I sent both of you a copy of the map."

"Where is the other map, the physical one you found?" Pete asked.

"Stored in a safe place. If it's authentic, it might be worth some ka-ching," Elvira said.

"So, if you don't find treasure, at least you can sell the map," Carlita said.

"It's an option." Elvira tapped Pete's arm. "The coding. You said you thought you recognized it and had some sort of translation document."

"Which I apparently misplaced or put in such a safe place I couldn't find it," he pointed out.

"Key word being couldn't." Elvira's eyes lit. "You found it, didn't you?"

"Maybe," Pete hedged.

"I knew it." Elvira whooped. "We are onto something now."

"Maybe. Maybe not." Pete studied the photo Elvira had forwarded. "It's what I thought."

"Please tell me you recognize the weird symbols."

"Possibly."

Elvira rolled her eyes. "You're killing me, here."

"Again. We're in the exploration phase," Pete warned. "Many others have already searched these tunnels. The treasure or treasures could be long gone."

"Nothing ventured. Nothing gained. Let's get cracking." Elvira turned to go. Carlita stopped her. "What else do you have inside your backpack?"

"Stuff," she answered evasively.

"What sort of stuff?"

"Some small tools, a portable metal detector, moisture meter and a compass."

Carlita craned her neck, gauging the weight of the woman's bag. "What about detonation devices?"

"Pete said no explosives."

"Being told no has never stopped you before."

Elvira heaved a heavy sigh. "Do you know you can be exasperating at times?"

"Look in the mirror," Carlita shot back.

"There are no explosives inside my backpack. I have a couple of other things, but that's it." Elvira made a cross on her chest. "Cross my heart."

"Fine," Pete said. "I won't search your bag. You had better be telling me the truth."

"Can I go now?" Elvira asked.

"Be my guest." Carlita started to follow and noticed her husband lingered, staring at his phone. "You think this might lead to something?" she whispered.

"It's possible," Pete said. "I studied my translation document. There's a good chance we have a match."

Elvira reappeared. "Are you guys coming?"

"Yes. We're coming." Pete lowered his voice. "She had better not have explosives."

"I wouldn't put anything past her," Carlita said. "Which is why we need to make sure we don't let Elvira out of our sight."

Chapter 12

They got to the bottom of the stairs, and Pete took the lead. The trio walked single file, keeping close to the right side to avoid the dip in the center of the tunnel.

Carlita ran a light hand across the brick wall, feeling the damp coolness. "These bricks almost feel wet."

"We're close to the river," Pete said. "The walls have felt cold and damp for as long as I can remember."

"But they aren't in imminent danger of collapsing?" Carlita asked.

"No. One would think the labyrinth of tunnels crisscrossing, backtracking and going in all different directions would eventually lead to structural issues, but whoever constructed them obviously knew what they were doing."

"These babies were built to last." Elvira patted the bricks. "Just look at how many times I've hammered away at my walls."

"Jackhammered, chipped away, blew out," Carlita said. "You're right. If anyone's walls and tunnels were going to go down, it would be Elvira's."

"Which is why I have a structural engineer on speed dial," she said. "Stuart Wempley knows his stuff."

"Stuart Wempley," Pete repeated. "I've heard his name before."

"Maybe he's inspected your tunnels."

"No. I've had them checked, but not by him."

They reached the main door with metal bars. Using his key, Pete unlocked the door. They continued walking until reaching an intersection.

He paused. "I haven't been beyond this point in quite some time."

Elvira spun in a slow circle. "I've been in this general area before."

"I'm sure you have," Pete sighed. "Straight ahead runs parallel to the river. If we turn right, we'll be going right toward it."

She muttered something unintelligible under her breath and then spoke loudly. "Do you own this part of the tunnel?"

"Yes."

"I'm gonna come clean. I've been down here."

"Chipping away or blowing walls out?" Carlita asked.

"No." Elvira abruptly stopped. "I have respect for other people's property."

"Really?" Carlita arched a brow. "Since when?"

"Since I didn't know who owned certain portions, not to mention I don't think the city would be too keen to find out I've been exploring without written consent."

"Ya think?" Pete asked sarcastically. "Let's keep moving."

They turned right. The tunnel pathway narrowed. The ceilings became lower, to the point Pete had to hunch down while Carlita could reach up and place her hand flat against the ceiling. "I feel like I'm going down Alice in Wonderland's rabbit hole."

"You wouldn't want to be down here if you were claustrophobic," Elvira said.

Pete stopped when they reached another door. Instead of metal with bars you could see through, this one was solid steel with rusty rivets securing the center panels. He fished a skeleton key from his pocket and inserted it in the lock.

"Hot diggity dog." Elvira licked her lips. "I figured there had to be a key somewhere around here."

Pete's eyes narrowed. "I see fresh scratches on this keyhole." He spun around, pinning Elvira with a stare. "When is the last time you were down here?"

"Not...long ago."

"Did you try picking this lock?"

Her eyes slid to the side. "Maybe."

"Elvira Cobb." Pete gritted his teeth. "This is private property."

"I wasn't sure who owned it. Had I known, I would have asked for permission. So, I'm guessing because you have the key, what's beyond this door belongs to you."

"The tunnel runs next to the Parrot House." Pete stepped to the left. "Two inches beyond this wall is city property. This side, from the edge of the door and right, all the way back to the Parrot House, is part of my property."

"Are you sure?"

"Positive. I have the survey to prove it."

"Interesting." Elvira's eyes flitted from side to side, and Carlita could see the wheels spinning.

"What would it entail? A city block? Two city blocks?"

"A substantial chunk of real estate." Pete unlocked the door. It creaked loudly as he eased it open. "Like I said, I haven't been down here in a while. Let me go first."

Carlita handed him the flashlight. He turned it on and cautiously stepped through the doorway.

Elvira nudged her out of the way and followed close behind him, leaving her to bring up the rear.

Much to Carlita's relief, the tunnel didn't narrow again. In fact, the ceilings were higher, much higher than the previous section, although the air was damper, as if it desperately needed a breath of fresh air. "Where is this taking us?" she finally asked.

"We have a little farther to go." Pete glanced over his shoulder. "Are you all right?"

"I'm fine. Although if I was gonna develop claustrophobia, it would hit right about now." Carlita could see a wall straight ahead. It was still a good twenty yards from them. "You sure this is safe?"

"Yes. It's been here for a very long time. We've almost reached the end." Pete continued walking.

"This is awesome," Elvira said. "Thank you for partnering with me, Pete. I mean, we haven't found anything yet, but I have a good feeling, like we're close to something big. These tunnels were built for a reason."

"They were built to transport stuff."

"Bodies. Yeah, I know."

"Bodies?" Carlita made a choking sound.

"During the Yellow Fever outbreak," Pete said. "They moved the bodies through the tunnels."

She shivered involuntarily. "I believe I may have heard the story, although it becomes more real when you're down here." Carlita warily eyed the walls, wondering how many bodies had passed through there.

She lowered her gaze, carefully skirting a dip in the floor.

Elvira spun around, her hands flying up in the air. "Boo!"

Carlita stumbled back and caught herself, inadvertently scraping her arm on the rough bricks. "Ack!"

"Gotcha." Elvira cackled. "Man, you should've seen the look on your face."

"Not funny." Carlita made a fist and punched her in the arm. "Don't scare me again."

Elvira frowned and rubbed her arm. "I was only trying to lighten the mood."

"You can be so annoying."

Pete nudged Elvira aside, concern etched on his face. "Are you okay?"

"Yes. Other than fighting the urge to knock some sense into Elvira." Carlita lifted her arm, revealing a minor scrape on her elbow. "If I end up with some sort of bacterial infection, it's all your fault."

Elvira waved dismissively. "It's nothing a little peroxide can't take care of."

Pete jabbed his finger at her. "Behave yourself or I'm going to escort you right back out of here and will never allow you in this area again."

"We have a deal."

"Which means nothing if it's not in writing. Stop with your antics." He leaned in, so close that their noses were only inches apart. "Understood?"

"Comprende." Elvira whispered something else under her breath.

"What did you say?"

"Nothing." She made a zipping motion across her lips. "Not a peep."

"That's what I thought." Pete took the lead again and continued walking until they reached the end.

Starting in the top right-hand corner and on his side of the tunnel, he beamed the flashlight down to the floor.

"What are you doing?" Elvira asked.

"Looking."

"For what?"

"Something."

"What sort of something?"

He motioned for her to step aside. She reluctantly complied.

Working his way back, Pete moved the flashlight up. Down. Up. Down, covering every square inch until he was roughly halfway between the solid metal door and the wall.

"I was almost sure I saw it here." Pete knelt on the ground and ran his fingertips along the edge.

Elvira dropped to her knees. "This reminds me of the hollowed-out spot in the tunnel by my house."

"Where you found the chest with your map and the silver coin?" Carlita asked.

"Correctamundo. I'm getting the same feeling in my gut."

"Maybe it's gas," Pete joked.

"Maybe. But I don't think so."

He grew quiet as he pulled his cell phone from his pocket. He clicked on the map Elvira had forwarded and enlarged a portion of it, the one showing a crude drawing of a three-sided shadow box with a long strip of metal. Three stars were above the metal strip.

"Will you look at this? All these years of owning this place."

"They're tiny," Carlita pointed out. "I can't imagine anyone finding them unless they were specifically looking for carvings. What is it?"

"A pirate symbol for gold."

"How do you figure?" Elvira leaned in. "I researched every single drawing on the map and found no indication of there being any gold."

"Are you a pirate?" Pete asked.

"No."

"I know what I'm looking at." He shifted the flashlight's beam, illuminating a matching symbol carved into the brick. Small, almost miniscule, yet there.

The color drained from Elvira's face. "We have a match."

Chapter 13

Pete was prepared for Elvira's reaction, which was to try shoving him out of the way. He held his ground, refusing to budge.

"Let me at it," she whined. "It's my map."

"And this is my wall."

"Actually, it isn't your map," Carlita pointed out. "You found it behind a wall owned by the City of Savannah."

"It's a technicality. I found the map. Finders keepers."

"Unless someone tells the city about it."

Elvira's jaw dropped. "You wouldn't rat me out."

"I would if you start acting like you own the place. This is Pete's wall. Therefore, the carving is also his and whatever else might be on this side of the tunnel."

Elvira scrambled to the other side. She turned her headlamp on high beam and began scouring the bricks.

Meanwhile, Pete continued examining the wall on his side.

Carlita switched her cell phone on and clicked on the map Elvira had texted her. Moving in the opposite direction and to Pete's left, she began searching for similar symbols.

Almost exactly two feet away and near the bottom, she found another symbol. This one didn't match one from Elvira's map but was a miniature replica of a pirate ship.

She tapped him on the shoulder and pointed to the carving. Pete glanced over at Elvira, who had already worked her way toward the end of the tunnel, all the while muttering under her breath.

Pete flashed his light over the spot. "Good eye."

"Good eye?" Elvira stopped what she was doing and scurried toward them. "You found something else?"

"Yes. It appears to be a pirate ship."

"I can't believe it." Elvira sucked in a breath and pressed her hand to her chest. "Finally. After all this time. After all my hours of hard work, the money, my pain and suffering, I might finally find treasure."

"We," Pete corrected. "We might have found something."

"We. Me. Same thing."

"No, it's not," Carlita said. "This is Pete's property."

"Let's not squabble over minor details." Elvira scooched forward. "I couldn't find anything on the other side, which means if there is something down here and based on the symbols you're finding, it would be on this side."

"It stands to reason," Pete agreed.

"What part of the wall still needs to be checked out?"

"The section to the right, closer to the steel door."

Elvira made a move to head in that direction and abruptly stopped.

"What is it?" Carlita asked.

"Why do you guys get to search the good section?"

She blinked rapidly, silently counting to ten. "What do you mean...the good section?"

"The better search spot."

"This is ridiculous." Pete shot his wife a look of aggravation. "Fine. You and Carlita can cover this area. I'll start over by the door."

"Sweet." Elvira squatted down, humming under her breath as she perused the bricks in her section, while Carlita continued her search. Moments later, she found another crude carving. "I found another one."

Pete returned and crouched down next to her. "It looks like a body of water, a riverbank." He ran his fingernail along the top. "My first thought is it looks like the moon overhead."

"I agree."

Tink. Tink.

A tinking noise echoed from the vicinity of the section Elvira was examining. Her back was to them, blocking their view.

Pete marched over. He reached down and snatched something out of her hand. "What is this?"

"It's a chipper."

"You're not supposed to be tinkering with the walls."

Elvira's brows knitted. "You told me no explosives. You didn't say anything about chipping away at the wall."

"No chipping, hammering, hacking, sawing, whacking or blowing up," Pete said. "We all agreed we're exploring, not excavating."

"Sheesh." Elvira started to reply and wisely changed her mind.

"I'm guessing you found something," he said.

"I did." She reluctantly showed him a crude carving of a treasure chest. "X marks the spot."

"I found another one." Carlita showed them a carving of a coin, this one farther up, at almost eye level. "This appears to be an area of significance."

"I agree." Pete stepped back, surveying the wall. "Now, what to do about it?"

"Take action. We need to figure out what's behind here." Elvira unzipped her backpack and began digging around. She pulled out a square black box with a reflective yellow strip at the top and placed it flat against the wall.

Blip. Blip.

"What is that?"

"A concrete scanner."

Blip. Blip.

"It will tell us if there are any hollow spots behind this brick." Elvira went into a long spiel, explaining how the device worked. "Basically, it uses a radio signal to bounce back waves, indicating whether you have solid material behind the wall, or an open area."

Blip. Blip.

"So far, this spot is solid." Elvira stepped to the left and placed it in another spot.

Blip. Blip.

She took another step.

Weep...weep...weep. The device blared loudly, "weeping" almost nonstop.

"This is it." Elvira's hand shook as she pulled the device away from the wall. "There's a hollow spot."

"It could be the ground settling," Pete said.

"Okay, doubting Dolly. Let's keep trying." Elvira took another step and placed the device flat against the brick.

Weep...weep...weep. The device detected another hollow spot. She continued working her way toward the end. Each stop indicated a hollow spot, nearly half the length of the tunnel. She reached the end, and it began "blipping" again.

Backtracking, Elvira tested the wall in the other direction, making her way toward the solid metal door.

The device continued to "weep...weep." The more it "weeped" the more Carlita became convinced there was a hollow space—a very large one—on the other side of the tunnel wall.

Elvira finished testing, a triumphant look on her face. "I haven't been this excited since I found the map and coin in the wall."

"What's our next step?" Carlita asked.

"It's a no-brainer. We take down the wall."

"No." Pete lifted a hand. "We're not doing anything, at least not yet."

"What do you mean?"

"I want to get an engineer back down here to examine the area and make sure taking the wall apart won't affect my restaurant's stability," Pete said.

"But…"

He cut Elvira off. "No buts. We're going to do this my way. I'll try to reach the engineer I hired some time ago to take a look at it."

"No need." Elvira waved her phone in the air. "Remember when I said I had my structural engineer Stuart Wempley on speed dial? I wasn't kidding."

Chapter 14

Elvira was a woman on a mission. Not only did she track down her structural engineer, but she also finagled a promise from him to stop by Pete's restaurant the following day to take a look at the tunnel before ending their call.

"I guess we're at a standstill." Elvira tapped her chin thoughtfully and spun in a slow circle.

"I don't like the look on your face," Carlita said.

"What look?"

"Like you're figuring out a way to sneak down here and start taking down walls before your guy checks it out."

"Nah. I've learned my lesson about messing with structural stuff. It's best to let the experts determine what's safe and what's not."

Carlita placed a hand on her hip. "I'm impressed. This is the most sensible thing to come out of your mouth in weeks."

"Maybe even months," Pete joked.

"Older and wiser," she said. "I have enough to keep me busy until tomorrow. Speaking of which, I tracked down the list of festival vendors and have the name of the Candy Cart's owner."

"You did? Wonderful."

"What is Candy Cart?" Pete asked.

Carlita briefly filled him in. "The bottom line is, we're wondering if the food truck is a front for something else. It's busier than any other vendor, not to mention Natalie was chatting with the employees shortly before her death."

"And their food tastes like crap," Elvira said. "It's not edible."

"You think Natalie knew or was somehow connected to the candy truck?"

"Correct. What's the owner's name?"

"Edward Stockton," Elvira said.

Carlita repeated it. "Did you find anything else out about him?"

"No." Elvira rubbed her thumb and fingers together. "I tracked down the name as a favor for a friend. Diving into a full-fledged investigation is gonna cost you."

"I have a computer. I can do some digging around."

"I don't mind helping, but I have bills to pay."

"I completely understand, and thank you for the name. Do you know if he's a local?" Carlita waved dismissively. "Never mind. I know how to find out. Actually, I should have done this before I left the festival earlier."

"Because the permit information is posted on the side of the food truck," Pete guessed. "The company name and contact information."

"Precisely." Carlita consulted her watch. "It's still early. I think I'll swing back by and snap a picture of their permit."

"Good luck with that," Elvira said.

"What do you mean?"

"The Candy Cart is packed from the minute they open until they close for the day. Someone will notice you taking a picture of their information."

"So? Maybe I'm a disgruntled customer who wasn't happy with my purchase."

"Which wouldn't be a stretch by any means," Elvira said. "However, something tells me if these people are involved in illegal activities, they won't appreciate you snooping around."

"Elvira has a valid point," Pete said. "I have a group outing on board The Flying Gunner. If we leave now, I can accompany you."

"Luigi is still over there working. He'll help you get what you need."

"Good idea," Carlita said. "No one will mess with Luigi."

The trio backtracked through the tunnel, pausing when they reached the heavy-duty metal door so Pete could lock it.

"My engineer is going to need access to this area." Elvira slid her phone out of her pocket and turned it on. "I need to pin him down to get an exact time."

The two went back and forth for several moments until finally agreeing on a window of time. "The best guesstimate is he'll be here around ten tomorrow morning."

Carlita did a mental calculation. "The timing should work, at least for me."

"The sooner we get the formalities out of the way, the sooner we can figure out what's behind the wall." Elvira made a beeline for the restaurant's main entrance, pausing when they reached the porch. "I'll see you at ten then."

Pete and Carlita lingered, watching her trudge off.

"Elvira will want to move full steam ahead as soon as the engineer gives us the green light," Carlita sighed.

"Her enthusiasm is equally concerning and contagious," Pete said. "There's no denying a link between the carvings on the tunnel bricks and the drawings on her map."

"If you think about it, it makes sense. Elvira found the map in a spot only a hop, skip, and jump from here." Carlita shifted her feet. "What if there is buried treasure...has been buried treasure right under your feet for all these years?"

"I'm not going to get my hopes up, unlike Elvira. We'll have to see how this plays out." Pete grasped Carlita's hand and placed a light kiss on top. "Will you be home for dinner tonight?"

"Of course." Carlita scooched closer. "How could I forget Sunday night is our designated date night? What would you like me to make?"

"Nothing." He pressed a light finger to her lips. "I'll handle dinner."

She placed her hands on both sides of his face, a soft smile playing on her lips as their eyes met. "Have I told you how much I love you?"

"Yes, but I'll never get tired of hearing it."

"I love you, Pete Taylor. You're a brave man for taking on the Garlucci family."

"And you're an equally brave woman to try to tame an old pirate."

Carlita reluctantly pulled away. "I suppose I had better get over to the festival and track down the Candy Cart's information."

"Be careful," Pete warned. "You don't know who you're dealing with."

"Not yet, but hopefully soon."

*****

Carlita ran upstairs to their apartment and grabbed Rambo. She and her pup took a leisurely stroll through Morrell Park, circling around the Waving Girl Statue, which was surrounded by a gaggling group of tourists, snapping pictures and meandering along the river.

Off in the distance, she glimpsed the ferry, transporting passengers to Hutchinson Island. They lingered near the railing, and her eyes were drawn toward the Parrot House Restaurant.

The landmark restaurant was mere steps away from the river. Was it possible a pirate ship went down in the river and ended up buried near the infamous pirate hangout? Pete had mentioned missing treasure on several occasions. What if it was nearby?

The idea there might actually be something to the enduring legend brought up a potential set of concerns. If some sort of treasure existed, who would it belong to? The City of Savannah? The state government? Pete?

The thought of a long-lost ship and treasure would attract archaeologists and curiosity-seekers. It would uproot not only Pete's business, but their personal lives, considering the couple lived above the restaurant.

One day at a time, Carlita reminded herself. *You have enough on your plate without worrying about the what ifs.* She called Rambo, who was in the thick of a meet and greet with a group of admirers.

They continued on a straight path along the main thoroughfare before cutting down a side street. Carlita and Rambo reached Freedom Square, slipped through the open gate and strolled along the sidewalk.

The square was filled with art aficionados, their arms laden with treasures purchased from one of the many talented artists. A piece of art caught her eye. It was a watercolor of the Parrot House

Restaurant, a replica and re-creation of what was now her home.

"It's one of my favorite pieces—among the top five I've ever created."

Carlita turned to find a young woman, in her late twenties or early thirties, if she had to guess, standing nearby. "I'm tempted to buy it."

"Have you ever visited the Parrot House Restaurant?"

Carlita grinned. "You could say I have...a time or two."

"It's one of my favorite restaurants." The woman leaned in. "A friend told me there's a tunnel beneath it. I've been tempted to sneak down there."

Carlita's expression grew mischievous. "I wouldn't if I were you," she whispered loudly. "I heard one curiosity seeker sneaked into the tunnel and disappeared."

The woman made a choking sound. "You're kidding. Did they...ever find them?"

"Actually, I *am* kidding." Carlita shifted Rambo's leash to her other hand. "I'm Carlita Taylor. Pete Taylor, the owner of the Parrot House, is my husband."

Her eyes widened. "I thought you looked familiar. You also own Ravello's Italian Eatery over in Walton Square."

"I do." Carlita unzipped her purse. "Pete and I live in an apartment above his restaurant. I have the perfect spot for this piece. How much is it?"

"Six hundred and twenty-five dollars. I love the idea of selling the piece to the owner. I'll sell it to you for five hundred, even."

"I hate to see you sell it at such a deep discount, considering the time and effort you put into ensuring it looks so much like the restaurant. Why don't we meet in the middle? I'll give you five hundred and sixty for it."

"It's a deal."

Carlita grabbed her pen and checkbook and wrote out a check. "It's a magnificent piece. As I mentioned, I have the perfect spot for it."

"Thank you." The woman tucked the check in her pocket. "Give me a couple of minutes to wrap it for you and attach a removal strap. It will make lugging it home a lot easier."

While the artist wrapped Carlita's purchase, they chatted about the festival and she pointed out her food truck off in the distance. "If you're in the mood for Italian, we have some delicious spaghetti and meatballs."

She patted her stomach. "I've already been by there. Twice. The food is delicious."

Carlita took the wrapped piece of art and thanked her.

Rambo, who had been sniffing around, trotted over and nudged her hand.

"Your dog is adorable."

"Thanks. Rambo is a real ham." Carlita lifted her purchase. "And thank you for the discount." She turned to go.

"Wait." The young artist stopped her. "I'm curious. Have you heard the rumor the restaurant is haunted?"

"Perhaps a time or two. Although I've never run across anything creepy or spooky." Carlita juggled Rambo's leash and her artwork. "I believe you can tour parts of the tunnel, although the section beneath the Parrot House isn't one of them."

"Have you been down there?"

Carlita thought about her earlier visit with Pete and Elvira. "Yes. It's dark, damp, and if you're even slightly claustrophobic, you might find it uncomfortable. It's not very exciting."

"I see." It was clear the woman was disappointed by Carlita's description. As she walked away to go search for Luigi, she silently added, *not very exciting unless there's a pirate ship or treasure just waiting to be found.*

Chapter 15

Carlita circled the square and finally found Luigi standing over by the center fountain. "C'mon, Rambo. I see Luigi."

She stepped in behind him and lightly tapped him on the shoulder.

He spun around. "Hey, Mrs. GT."

Carlita chuckled. "Hello, Luigi. Elvira mentioned you were still working here at the festival. I need your help."

"She already called. Said you wanted to get the 411 on the Candy Cart."

"I do. I'm looking for information about the owner."

"Are you thinking about partnering with them? Cuz if you are, I wouldn't recommend it. Their food is disgusting. I tried a bag of caramel corn. It was like eating a box of mothballs."

"Yuck." Carlita curled her lip. "I've heard their food isn't good."

"Isn't good is an understatement. Anyway, I figured I would warn you they might not be a good business partner if you were looking to team up."

"Mercedes and I remember seeing Natalie Lameron, the deceased woman, hanging around there the other day. We're wondering if the candy is used as a cover and they're actually selling drugs."

"Makes sense." Luigi pulled a cigarette from his pocket, lit the end, and took a long drag. "They're busier than anybody else around here. I was wondering what was up. People would be crazy to keep going back."

"I think there might be a link between Natalie and someone associated with the Candy Cart."

"Which is why you're lookin' to get their info. So you can check 'em out."

"Bingo."

Luigi dangled the cigarette from his lips and patted Rambo's head. "You know where they post a copy of the permit?"

"Yes. On the side. Same as ours, although I'm not sure which one."

"I'll do a quick check for you and be right back." Luigi took another drag on his cigarette and sauntered across the square, making a beeline for the Candy Cart.

Carlita watched him circle the food truck. He gave her a slight nod of the head. Catching his drift, she and her pup zig zagged past several trucks and caught up with him near the entrance. "Did you find it?"

"Yeah. It's on the left-hand side if you're facing the counter."

"Thank you. I'll snap a quick pic and be on my way." Carlita turned to go. Luigi stopped her. "If they're getting action, they got eyes on all sides of their heads."

"Meaning they'll be on the lookout for suspicious behavior."

"Like snapping pictures. You could be putting a target on your back, you know?"

"If they're running a drug dealing business from the food truck, they'll be keeping a close eye on who comes and goes."

"Exactly." Luigi took one last drag off his cigarette and flicked it on the ground. "I got an idea. I noticed they have a flat tire. I'm gonna lure them to the front of the trailer while you slip around to the other side. You gotta move fast cuz we'll only have a few seconds."

"Right." Carlita reached into her pocket and pulled out her cell phone.

"As soon as you see them following me, get what you need and move out."

"Got it." Carlita gave him a thumbs up. "Thanks, Luigi. I appreciate your help."

"You're welcome. I gotta keep on my landlady's good side," he joked.

"We're family," Carlita said. "I'm no longer just your landlady."

"And the best family a former mobster could ask for." Luigi cut back across the square and walked straight to the window.

Carlita slowly trailed behind, watching as the workers exited the trailer and followed him to the side.

Moving quickly, she and Rambo darted to the left. Carlita located the permit and snapped a picture. She glanced at the blurry photo.

"Crud." She took a deep breath, steadied her hand and snapped a second picture, this one clear as a bell. She tucked her phone in her pocket and spun around, nearly colliding with a man wearing a "Candy Cart" logoed shirt.

She stumbled back, her heart racing. "I'm sorry. I didn't see you."

"What are you doing back here?"

"My dog. I was looking for a place for him to go to the bathroom."

"Find another spot," the man growled. "We have food and supplies back here. We don't need a dog sniffing around. It's bad for business."

"Right. Right. I apologize." Carlita inched back, tugging on Rambo's leash.

The pup let out a warning growl and bared his teeth.

"Get your dog out of here." The man lifted his leg, intending to kick Rambo.

"C'mon, Rambo." Carlita hurriedly led him out of the area. The hair on the back of her neck stood up, and she knew the man was watching her. "Luigi wasn't kidding when he said they would be guarding their goods."

Carlita headed home and then decided to drive over to Ravello's so she could check on Mercedes. She parked in the alley, circled around to the front and found her daughter waiting on tables.

She lingered near the server's station until she was free. "How's it going?"

"Okay. Sam sent a text early this afternoon asking how I was doing," Mercedes said. "I told him I was fine and hoped he was, too."

"Did he mention anything else?"

"Yeah. He said he was going to run by the police station this afternoon to get an update on Natalie's case."

"If anyone can get the scoop, it'll be Sam," Carlita said.

"Except for the fact he's also involved." Mercedes changed the subject. "How did it go with Elvira and the tunnel?"

"We found some carvings on the wall. They match a few of the ones on the map Elvira found."

"Seriously?" Mercedes pressed a hand to her chest. "So you might actually be onto something with the whole pirate tunnel theory?"

"Possibly. Elvira brought a tool with her. It detected a hollow spot behind the tunnel wall."

"I bet she was ready to knock it down."

"Knock it down. Blow it up. Sledgehammer it out," Carlita said. "Her structural engineer is coming by tomorrow to check it out, to find out if it's safe to start tinkering."

"Imagine finding treasure."

"Like the gems we found in our basement. Not only is Savannah full of rich history, but it might also be full of rich something else." Carlita patted her pocket. "I have some info on the Candy Cart. Edward Stockton is the owner."

"Edward Stockton," Mercedes repeated. "His name doesn't ring a bell."

"It doesn't to me either. Rambo and I went by the food truck and snapped a picture of the permit."

"So we can research the company's name and address?"

"Bingo," Carlita said. "How much longer are you working?"

"About an hour."

"I have some bookwork to do. The food truck has eaten up a lot of our inventory. I'm pretty sure we're getting low on some stuff." Carlita promised to hang around until Mercedes finished her shift and then she and Rambo headed to the office in the back.

"There's my buddy." McKenna, one of Ravello's servers and Rambo's biggest fan, ran over to greet him. "I bought Rambo a toy. Do you mind if we go out to my car and grab it?"

"Not at all."

Rambo happily trotted after his friend while Carlita settled in at the desk. She logged into the restaurant's site and ran an inventory report. As suspected, they were low on several key items.

She promptly placed an order and scheduled the delivery before checking her emails and going over the staffing schedule.

Carlita was thrilled with the success of the food truck, but it also meant she was stretching her resources. In other words, she wasn't sure if she would continue taking part in the festivals unless she could hire additional workers to cover all the venues.

The time passed quickly. Before she knew it, Mercedes trudged into the kitchen. "Hey, Ma."

Carlita turned, giving her daughter her full attention. "Are you clocked out?"

"Yeah. I'm ready to get off my feet."

"I don't blame you." Carlita exited the computer screens. She gathered her papers and she and Rambo followed Mercedes out into the alley for the short walk to the apartment.

Mother and daughter climbed the stairs and reached the landing, where they found Sam's door ajar.

Carlita jabbed her finger in that direction and pointed at Mercedes, who shook her head. She slipped her key in the lock and opened the door.

Rambo scrambled around them and ran inside.

"Rambo," Carlita scolded.

Mercedes laughed. "He's home."

"Crazy dog."

"Hey!"

The women turned to find Sam standing in his doorway.

Carlita discreetly slipped past her daughter, planning to go inside to give them privacy.

Sam stopped her. "Don't go, Carlita. I dropped by the station on my way home to see if there was any new information about Natalie's case."

"And?" Carlita clasped her hands, offering up a small prayer for a miracle that the police had apprehended the woman's killer.

"Things aren't looking good."

Chapter 16

"Detective Polivich doesn't have a clue who murdered Natalie," Carlita guessed.

"Oh, he's definitely leaning in one direction," Sam said. "Actually, he's leaning in two."

"Yours and mine," Mercedes said.

"Yep. Other than her killer, we were the last ones to see Natalie alive. Polivich went poking around over at Sandy Sue's Bar-B-Que across the street and found an eyewitness, an employee, who claims he saw Natalie over here talking to us."

"More like arguing," Mercedes said.

"Correct. The employee also claims he thought he witnessed a physical altercation."

"When Natalie tried scratching you."

"According to the employee, he wasn't able to see who went after who, only that it became physical."

"Great," Carlita groaned. "So now the cop is thinking you and Mercedes ganged up on Natalie and took her out."

"He didn't come right out and admit it, but it's clear Polivich will be focusing on us. My guess is he also plans to swing by the news station and chat with Autumn, who was around when it happened."

"She was in the courtyard and too far away to hear what was being said," Mercedes pointed out.

"I disagree. She can corroborate what she knows. I talked to Tony earlier. He said Polivich stopped by the pawn shop."

"He took prints from one of the guns in the display case," Carlita said. "Tony is almost certain Natalie and a guy who came in around the same time were together."

"Unless there's a database match, the fingerprints won't help us." Sadie circled Sam's legs. "I need to take Sadie out. Would you like to go with us? Maybe get a little fresh air," he hinted.

"No thanks. Ma and I have some stuff we're looking into." Mercedes turned on her heel and walked into the apartment.

Sam's shoulders drooped as he watched her walk away. "I sure messed up."

"Yes, you did," Carlita agreed. "I can't speak for my daughter, but if I were in her shoes, it would be a matter of trust. You didn't trust her enough to let her know what was going on."

"As I said before, you don't know Natalie. She would've gone after Mercedes."

Carlita cut him off. "Which she did. Maybe it would have been better for her to have a heads up. She's gonna need some time and space."

"It's the least I can do after getting us into this."

Carlita patted his arm. "Try not to be too hard on yourself. You thought you were protecting

Mercedes. It was the best of intentions with poor execution."

"In a nutshell. C'mon, Sadie. Let's go for a walk."

Carlita lingered for a long moment after Sam left. It was clear he thought he had done the right thing to protect Mercedes. She also knew the Garluccis were a stubborn bunch of Italians. The ball was now in her daughter's court and would stay there, at least for the time being.

*****

Mercedes waited for her mother to step inside the apartment and close the door behind her. "What did Sam say?"

"That he screwed up. He knows it and he's scrambling, trying to figure out how to fix the mess he made." Carlita dropped her purse on the table by the door and crossed the room.

Grayvie scampered over and arched his back, rubbing up against Carlita's legs.

She scratched his ears and told him what a good boy he was before pulling her phone from her pocket. "I have the information on the Candy Cart owner."

"Cuz you still think there's a link between them and Natalie?"

"I do." Carlita tracked down the photo of the food truck's permit. "I figured if you had a few minutes, we could do a little digging around to see what we can find out."

"Sounds good." Mercedes logged onto her laptop and opened a new search screen. "What do you have?"

"Candy Cart, 1512 County Line Road, Pooler, GA," Carlita said.

Mercedes typed the information in the search bar and hit enter. Several sites popped up. Working her way from top to bottom, she checked out each site she found. "It looks like it's owned by Edward

Stockton. The only address listed is the one on County Line Road."

Carlita grabbed the notes she'd started earlier at breakfast and jotted Candy Cart right below it. "Our next logical step is to find out what we can about the owner."

"Already on it." Mercedes' fingers flew over the keys. She bounced between LinkedIn and several other social media sites.

Carlita slipped her reading glasses on. "There's not much about Stockton."

"He has a social media page, but only a couple dozen followers." Mercedes skimmed the list, but nothing popped out as a lead. "It looks like he's pretty much abandoned it."

"Which could be because it's not legit," her mother said.

"True. If he's using the food truck as a front for drug dealings, I guess he wouldn't be interested in drumming up legitimate, legal business." Mercedes leaned back in her chair, thoughtfully tapping her chin.

"What are you thinking?"

"About ways to find out what's up with the Candy Cart."

"Meaning a sting, to see if they're selling drugs?"

"Yeah."

Carlita began shaking her head. "I don't like it. If this guy, Stockton, has drug ties, it could be dangerous. Maybe this is something Sam can help us figure out."

"I don't think it's wise to ask him," Mercedes said. "He's a former cop. I'm sure if there is something illegal going on, the dealers know who's who."

Her daughter had a point. If they detected even the slightest hint of police poking around, they would close ranks and act legit. Carlita thought about Luigi and immediately dismissed him. "Tony might be able to do some nosing around."

Mercedes pointed to herself. "What about me?"

"What about you?"

"I could try to buy drugs." Mercedes quickly warmed to the idea. "Think about it. Sure, the workers or dealers might have noticed us, but it's not a big deal."

Her mother wrinkled her nose. "I dunno."

"They won't dare do anything to me. The festival is in a public place with tons of people around. All I gotta do is try to buy something."

"Like what?"

"Let me text Sam." Mercedes snatched her phone off the counter and tapped out a brief message. "I'm asking him if he knew what kind of drugs Natalie was on."

Tink.

"That was fast." Mercedes opened the message. "He thinks it was pot and cocaine."

"You're gonna need to know the lingo," Carlita said. "You can't just waltz over there and tell them you want to buy some marijuana."

Mercedes began humming under her breath. "Four twenty. Four twenty is code for marijuana."

"So you're gonna mosey on over, go up to the counter and ask them for some four twenty?"

"Sure. Why not? I'll need to figure out how much this stuff costs." Mercedes let out a low whistle. "Wow. High-quality pot is over three hundred bucks an ounce. Middle grade stuff is over two. On the cheap end, it's around one hundred and forty dollars."

"It sounds like an expensive habit," Carlita said. "How much did Natalie say she needed to pay her dealer?"

"Fifteen hundred dollars. Maybe her drug debt was for cocaine." Mercedes started a new search, trying to get a rough estimate of the cost. "Now we're getting somewhere. From what I'm finding it looks like cocaine is more expensive."

"You'll need some cash," Carlita said. "We have to work at the food truck tomorrow at noon."

"Right. As soon as I have a break, I'll run over and try to buy some," Mercedes said. "I think she was high on cocaine the other night. She had several symptoms. High energy, talkative, mood swings, glassy eyes. Yeah, Natalie nailed the mood swing part. One minute, she was laughing and joking. The next she was crying and begging."

Carlita pressed her palms together. "I don't like the idea of you purchasing illegal drugs."

"Do you have a better idea? Natalie was talking to the food truck workers. If they're drug dealers, chances are one of them is the 'he' she owed money to."

"It stands to reason. Still..." An uneasiness settled over Carlita. It appeared they were on the right track. But if the Candy Cart was a cover for drug dealers, and one of the employees was Natalie's dealer, the person may have murdered the woman.

The thought of Mercedes trying to do business with them was more than a little worrisome. On the other hand, she had a valid point. The festival was packed. If the food truck employees were dealing drugs, they had customers making purchases all day. She would be just another customer.

"I'll be fine."

Carlita slowly stood. "I promised Pete I would be home for dinner."

Mercedes followed her mother to the door.

"Be careful if you're out and about tonight."

"It's been a long day. Grayvie and I will hang out here and watch television. Maybe I'll invite Autumn over." Mercedes held up a finger. "Before you go, take some slices of my chocolate peanut butter pie with you."

Carlita waited while Mercedes ran into the kitchen. She returned moments later with a to-go container in hand. "It's one of my best desserts to date."

"I can't wait to try it." Carlita hesitated. "Are you sure you're all right?"

"Yep. Go have a nice evening with Pete. I'll meet you out back at Ravello's in the morning."

"You got it. And call. Call if you need anything at all."

Mercedes accompanied her mother downstairs and let her out the back door. Carlita waited to hear the lock click in place before walking to her car. She coaxed Rambo into the front seat before placing the pie in the back.

She pulled out of the parking spot, her eyes drawn to Mercedes' balcony and the soft glow emanating from the living room light. "I sure hope we're able to figure something out soon."

Carlita's gut told her if they couldn't figure out who had murdered Sam's ex, her daughter, or Sam would stay at the top of the cop's list.

Chapter 17

Carlita wasn't surprised to find the Parrot House Restaurant's parking lot jampacked with the dinner crowd. She eased into her spot out back, right next to Pete's pickup.

Juggling her artwork and purse, she nudged Rambo inside before climbing the stairs leading to the apartment's private entrance.

The door was ajar. The soft sound of classical music greeted her in the hall.

"Hello?" Carlita smelled the enticing aroma of grilled meat. She wandered through the living room and found the sliding door leading to their penthouse's rooftop deck wide open.

The music grew louder, and she glimpsed her husband standing in front of the gas grill. Their corner bistro table for two sported a crisp white tablecloth. In the center was a vase containing three long-stemmed red roses.

"What's all this?" Carlita dropped her purse on the table and placed the pie and artwork next to it.

"Happy anniversary." Pete shut the lid on the grill and made his way over. He softly kissed Carlita's lips. "Don't tell me you forgot."

"Forgot what?"

"It's our three-month wedding anniversary." Pete placed a light hand on her arm. "I ordered a picture perfect sunset to go along with our special dinner."

"I'm sorry, Pete. I completely forgot with everything going on," she apologized.

"I understand."

"It's been hectic, juggling the food truck, the businesses, not to mention dealing with the death of Sam's ex." Carlita changed the subject. "What can I do to help?"

"I was working on setting the table. There's a dish of twice-baked potatoes in the oven, along with steamed corn on the cob and the most decadent sweet rolls I've ever had the pleasure of sinking my teeth into."

"I can't wait to try them. You finish cooking the meat and I'll set the table." Carlita worked quickly, carrying the dishes of food to the larger table, along with their elegant dinner plates, a set their friend Victoria "Tori" Montgomery had given them as a wedding gift.

She poured two sparkling waters, arranged the silverware and then lit a candle.

"Do you mind if Gunner joins us?" Pete carried the parrot's cage out onto the deck.

"Not at all."

"Gunner is handsome," the bird squawked.

"Yes, you are handsome," she agreed.

Rambo, who had been patrolling the kitchen and the deck, trotted out. He flopped down near Gunner's cage.

"Rambo is rude," the bird shrieked.

"Rambo is not rude," Carlita said.

"Gunner loves grapes."

Pete ran inside, grabbed a handful of grapes for Gunner and some treats for Rambo.

"Drop the gun or I'll shoot."

Carlita grinned. "Drop the gun? Gunner has added some new sentences to his repertoire."

"Unfortunately, I left reruns of Starsky and Hutch playing on the television while I was catching up on bookwork. Thus, the reason for Gunner's expanded vocabulary."

"Do me a favor and tip your hat forward," Gunner said.

"It's been nonstop all afternoon," Pete sighed. "I might have to put him back inside so we can have some peace and quiet during our meal."

"Don't make me shoot."

"I've heard enough." Pete carried Gunner back inside.

The couple filled their plates with grilled steak and sides before settling in to enjoy the setting sun. "Thank you for a delightful dinner."

"You're welcome." Pete lifted his glass. "A toast to our three-month anniversary."

Carlita lifted hers. "And to the most thoughtful husband a woman could ever ask for."

While they ate, they chatted about business, about the food truck, and then the conversation shifted to Natalie Lameron's murder. "Mercedes and I are seriously starting to suspect the Candy Cart is a front for selling drugs."

"It could be. You and Elvira both mentioned their food was terrible," Pete said.

"Inedible. Natalie was over there the day of her death. I'm not saying for sure they're selling drugs, but it could be."

"How do you propose to find out for sure?"

"We're working at the festival tomorrow. Mercedes is going to try buying some drugs."

Pete made a choking sound. "Buy drugs?"

"It sounds crazy, but she has her mind set. With our luck, the cops will do a drug bust and she'll get caught in an undercover sting."

"If they're legit drug dealers and linked to the woman's death, it could also be dangerous," Pete pointed out.

"I agree. Mercedes is acting like it isn't a big deal." Carlita toyed with her food, visions of her daughter being ambushed by cops or—worse yet—

taken out by a drug dealer / killer. "She seems to think being out in the open offers some protection."

"It could be," Pete agreed. "I know Mercedes well enough to know that when she sets her mind to something, she won't let it go."

"She comes by it rightfully, I suppose." Carlita blew air through thinned lips. "Sam swung by the police department. Detective Polivich spoke with one of Sandy Sue's employees, who witnessed the confrontation between Sam, Mercedes, and Natalie. He said it became physical."

"Is it true?"

"Natalie tried scratching Sam," Carlita said.

"Unfortunately, they'll be focusing solely on motive and opportunity, not to mention they have plenty of surveillance footage showing the woman behind your apartment building shortly before her body was found."

"Bingo. What if..."

"What if what?" Pete asked.

"Sam claims he was out walking Sadie when Natalie reappeared and lured Mercedes down to the alley. What if he was nearby and he confronted Natalie again. It got ugly, and she...died."

"You mean Sam killed her?" Pete mulled over the suggestion. "It's possible. I suppose if she came at him with a knife, he would be forced to defend himself."

"Which would mean Natalie's killer lives only steps away from my daughter."

Pete reached for her hand. "I don't know Sam as well as you do, but something tells me he didn't kill the woman."

"I don't want to believe it either." Carlita scooped up a forkful of her potato. "We need to save room for Mercedes' chocolate peanut butter pie."

"Then I had better stop now. The good news is we'll have leftovers for lunch."

While Pete put the food away, Carlita started a pot of coffee. She grabbed two dessert plates and transferred the slices from the container to the plates.

After the coffee finished brewing, she placed their cups and dessert on a tray and carried it outdoors.

Pete stood near the table, eyeing the wrapped piece of art. "What is this?"

"A surprise." Carlita eased the tray onto the table. "For you. Maybe somewhere in the cobwebbed recesses of my mind I remembered our anniversary after all," she joked. "Go ahead. Open it."

Pete carefully removed the tape securing the corners. He set the paper aside and studied the framed artwork. "This is awesome."

"Pretty cool, huh? I found it while I was scoping out the festival. As soon as I saw the painting, I knew we had to have it."

Pete tilted his head and grinned. "Did you happen to notice this?"

"Notice what?" Carlita leaned in.

"Gunner. He's in the corner."

Sure enough, Pete's parrot was perched on a pole near the corner of the porch.

"I have the perfect place for this."

"In the empty spot near the fireplace mantle," Carlita guessed.

"Yeah. You were thinking the same thing?"

"I was." Carlita waited for him to set it aside before handing him a fork. "I can't wait to try Mercedes' pie."

"It looks delicious."

Carlita carved out a small piece, savoring the creamy peanut butter mingled with a trace of bitterness from the dark chocolate. She took a bigger bite. "This is delicious," she murmured.

"It's one of the best peanut butter pies I've ever tasted." Pete tore into his decadent dessert, polishing his piece off in record time. "I could eat a whole pie."

"She only gave me two pieces." Carlita offered him the rest of hers. He politely declined. "Not a chance. You enjoy every morsel."

The couple lingered over a second cup of coffee before reluctantly making their way back inside.

"Hands up or I'll shoot," Gunner squawked. "Pretty girl at twelve o'clock."

"Carlita is beautiful," Pete said.

"Gunner is handsome," the parrot replied.

"Poor Rambo has to listen to Gunner's ramblings all day." Pete ruffled the pup's ears. "Although he doesn't seem to mind."

"I think he enjoys the company."

The couple rinsed their dishes off and placed them in the dishwasher.

Pete ran downstairs to grab a hammer and returned to hang their new piece of art on the wall. Carlita waited for him to finish and then deemed it a perfect fit for the empty spot.

She slipped her arms around his waist and leaned her head against his chest. "It's feeling more like home every day."

"Good. Because this *is* your home. I want you to add your woman's touch until you're tickled pink."

"Tickled pink," Gunner echoed.

"I wonder what tomorrow's forecast is showing." Carlita settled in next to him on the couch. "We've had some gorgeous weather for the festival."

"Let's check." Pete flipped through the stations until finding a local channel. The couple waited for the forecast. "It looks like it's going to be another beautiful day."

He started to change the channel when a news flash popped up at the top. Carlita's heart skipped a beat when she realized what it was. "Hang on. It looks like a story about Natalie's death."

They grew quiet, listening to the reporter fill viewers in on the case.

"If you're just tuning in, the Savannah Police Department is investigating the horrific murder of model and former local Natalie Lameron. Police found Ms. Lameron's body late last night in Walton Square."

A shot of a somber Polivich appeared, flanked by two uniformed officers.

"The case has taken an interesting turn."

Steps behind the officers were two other cops, both equally solemn. Carlita nearly hit the floor when she glimpsed the person who was handcuffed and walking between them. "Oh my gosh."

Chapter 18

Carlita stared at the television in disbelief, watching as a handcuffed Sam Ivey was escorted across a parking lot to the back of the downtown Savannah-Burnham Police Department.

"I wonder if Mercedes knows Sam's been arrested." She grabbed her phone and dialed her daughter's number.

"Hey, Ma. I was just getting ready to call you."

"The police arrested Sam."

"Yeah. They showed up on our doorstep about an hour ago." Mercedes' voice grew muffled. "Luigi, Dernice and Autumn are here."

"Do you have any idea what kind of evidence they have?"

"No, but Dernice said Elvira is calling her friend who works down at the station. She should have something soon."

"Pete and I are on the way."

"You don't..."

"We know, but we want to." Carlita told her they would be there shortly.

By the time she ended the call, Pete had already locked the slider, grabbed the truck keys and stood waiting by the door. "How is Mercedes holding up?"

"So far, so good. She sounds calm." Carlita shared what she knew on their way across town.

Using her key, she let them in through the back hall door. From the lower level, she could hear loud voices.

They climbed the stairs and found the apartment door ajar. Dernice, Luigi, Autumn, and Tony were inside with Mercedes.

"Where's Elvira?" Carlita asked.

"She should be here any minute," Mercedes said. "She was waiting to hear back from her contact who works at the police department."

"And Sam? Any news on Sam?"

"Speaking from experience, they're probably still booking him," Luigi said.

Sam's pup Sadie trotted over, and Carlita picked her up. "I was going to ask about Sadie."

"As soon as Sam was taken away, I went over and grabbed her." Mercedes paced. "This is awful."

"At least it wasn't you," Tony said.

"When I saw the cops pull into the alley, I figured they were after me." Mercedes placed a light hand on her forehead. "They must have some sort of solid evidence to get an arrest warrant."

The apartment door flew open. Elvira appeared. "Where's the party?"

"I wish," Carlita said. "And I'm sure Sam is wishing he was anywhere but downtown being booked."

"Were you able to find anything out?" Mercedes asked.

"Not only do I know what the cops found, I have a copy." Elvira waved a fistful of papers in the air. "The police found Natalie's car a couple of blocks from here."

Carlita's mind whirled. "There was something inside."

"Natalie's journal, among other things. My buddy works for the investigation team. He was on hand when they accessed her vehicle. He forwarded a few pictures." Elvira started to lay them out on the dining room table, changed her mind and snatched them back up. "This is confidential stuff. What I'm about to show you can't leave this room."

"Mum's the word," Mercedes said.

Elvira jabbed her finger in Autumn's direction. "This means you. You can't share any of this with your co-workers. In other words, no inside scoop for Channel 11 News."

"As much as I would love the story, friendship takes priority. If Sam is innocent, I want to help him, not make things worse," Autumn said.

"That's what I wanted to hear." Elvira placed the sheets of paper on the table while the others gathered around.

The first photos were different angles of the vehicle's exterior—a gray two-door convertible with a Florida license plate. The next few included one of the trunk, filled with clothes. Not neatly or tidily organized, but carelessly crammed inside.

There were several angles of the interior, in a similar state of disarray. Fast food bags, Starbucks cups, plastic cutlery, water bottles, some still half full. A travel bag and makeup case. Wet wipes, a pillow and blanket.

"Pillows and blankets," Dernice said. "She must have been living in her car."

"How sad," Autumn said. "Natalie was homeless."

"Living in her car and feeding her addiction." Carlita's throat clogged. Regardless of how troubled the woman may have been, it was a terrible way to live.

"I've been around plenty of people in similar situations," Luigi said. "First, they can't pay their rent, so they sell what they can and move into their vehicles. When they run out of money, they sell the vehicles and are forced to live on the streets."

"She was one step away from desperation," Autumn said.

"I think she had already reached the desperation phase," Mercedes said. "She was at the end of her rope and reached out to the only person she could think of who might help her—Sam."

"Which he did, and she took advantage of it," Pete said. "She's dead. Sam's in jail and her killer is on the loose."

Carlita studied the rest of the photos. "How does this prove Sam was the one who killed her? You said something about a journal."

"According to my source, it was mostly ramblings, consistent with someone who is mentally unstable, until the last entry." Elvira pulled a piece of paper from her pocket. "They found an entry from two days before her death when Natalie specifically mentioned being scared. Sam was angry with her and she felt threatened by him."

"What exactly did she write?" Mercedes asked.

Elvira cleared her throat. "Sam has agreed to meet with me one last time. I've never seen him so angry. He told me more than once he wants me out of his life forever. What if he tries to kill me?"

"Does she mention the drug dealer?" Carlita asked.

"I believe so, but only in passing," Elvira said. "Most of what was in her journal was weird ramblings, which made absolutely no sense."

"One of the few sane things she wrote about was being afraid of Sam." Mercedes blew air through thinned lips. "She also accused me of killing Sam right before she ran off."

Dernice twirled her finger next to her forehead. "Drugs will mess with your mind."

"So now what?" Autumn asked. "It looks like the police believe they have Natalie's killer."

"What if they're right?" Tony asked. "I hate to say it, but what if Sam killed her?"

"I can't…" Mercedes' voice faded.

Carlita put her arm around her daughter's shoulder. "We're going to stick with our plan."

Elvira perked up. "Plan?"

"To find out if the Candy Cart food truck is dealing drugs."

"You might be messing with some bad people," Tony warned.

"I agree," Carlita said. "However, we'll be in an open, public place. There's only so much they would do."

"Who's doing the sting?" Luigi asked.

"Me," Mercedes said.

"I'll be working at the festival again tomorrow. What time were you thinking?" he asked.

"Mercedes and I start our shift at noon. Probably after the lunch crowd thins. Maybe one-ish?"

"I'll be sure to patrol your area around one," Luigi promised.

Tony cleared his throat. "You sure you wanna try it? If they killed this chick, what's going to stop them from doing it again?"

"What other choice do we have?" Mercedes asked. "If they clear Sam, I'll be next. I would rather do my investigating outside of jail, not inside and behind bars."

Chapter 19

Pete and Carlita were the last to leave Mercedes' apartment, but not before their daughter reassured them she was fine. Despite the current state of affairs between her and Sam, she still believed he was innocent.

"You're sure you wanna go through with trying to figure out if the candy food truck is a front for drugs?" Carlita asked.

"One hundred percent. Sam didn't kill Natalie. I believe this with all my heart." Mercedes reminded her mother what Natalie had said, how it was too late and "he" was after her.

"True. If she thought Sam was going to take her out, the last thing she would do was ask him for more money," Carlita said. "Still, I have a bad feeling about this whole thing."

"I'm not getting warm and fuzzy either," Pete said. "If the drug dealer is involved in the woman's death, something tells me it might be part of a larger operation."

"Luigi promised to be nearby," Mercedes reminded them. "I won't make a move until he's around in case I run into trouble."

Feeling slightly mollified and knowing Luigi could handle almost anything thrown his way, Carlita let it drop.

Later that night, long after she crawled into bed, she tossed and turned, wondering how the woman had become tangled up in a life of drugs and reached the point where she was forced to live in her car. Despite the Garlucci family's illicit past, at least her children had never gotten into drugs and ended up on the streets.

Except for her son, Vinnie. Carlita was still worried about his chosen career path, marrying the daughter of Vito Castellini, the head of the mafia. Despite Vito's death, the "family" was alive and well on the East Coast, thanks in part to Vito's son Tommy, who had taken over.

On occasion, her son mentioned tensions between him and Tommy. Before Vito's death, he'd announced Vinnie as his successor, which caused more than a little animosity between the brothers-in-law.

Much to Carlita's relief, Vinnie had stepped back and let Tommy take over. Which meant although there would always be a target on Vinnie's back, he wasn't the number one target.

She still hoped one day Brittney, Vinnie and their young son would move away and start a new life, a life not involving the mafia.

Time and again, she'd reminded her son he would always have a place in the Garlucci family businesses, a career lucrative enough to allow him to provide for his family in Savannah. Perhaps not to the degree Vinnie and Brittney were accustomed to, but comfortable, nonetheless.

She awoke early the next morning. Bleary-eyed, Carlita shuffled out of the bedroom to start a pot of coffee. Pete wasn't far behind. He caught up with his wife in the kitchen and gave her a peck on the cheek. "Rough night, huh?"

"One of the worst." Carlita stifled a yawn. "First, I was hot. Then I was cold. Then I had to go to the bathroom, which was right around the time Rambo decided he needed a potty break."

The coffee finished brewing. Carlita poured two cups and handed him one. "What's on your schedule for the day?"

"I'm meeting a repair guy at the pirate ship at eight to fix the leak. I'm pretty sure I figured out where it's coming from. Hopefully, it's a small repair. I'll be sure to be back here by ten."

"What's at ten?"

"Elvira and her structural engineer," Pete said.

"You're right. I completely forgot about her having her guy inspect your tunnel."

"I can guarantee she didn't."

Carlita sipped her coffee, eyeing her husband over the rim. "What if he gives the green light to tearing out a section of the tunnel wall?"

"Then I guess we find out what's behind it. Maybe." Pete rubbed the stubble on his chin. "I have to admit, I'm curious. I see too many similarities between the map markings and carvings on the wall. We know for a fact there's been plenty of treasure buried around Savannah. I suppose it's entirely possible not all of it has been found."

"Because of the old tale about a sunken pirate ship," Carlita said.

"Which was never recovered." Pete downed the rest of his coffee and headed to the bathroom to get ready. After finishing, he swapped places with his wife. She made quick work of showering and grabbed Rambo's leash on their way out.

Pete parted ways with them at the bottom of the stairs, but not before reminding her about the ten o'clock meeting in the tunnel.

The air was crisp and cool, and Carlita savored the quiet of an early Monday morning. Despite being thrilled by how well the food truck had done over the weekend, she was looking forward to serving a lighter crowd.

She let Rambo take the lead, walking at a brisk pace through the center of Morrell Park. They reached the other side and cut across the street, passing by the Book Nook and Colby's Corner Store. Turning left, they slowed when they reached Shades of Ink, Steve Winter's tattoo shop.

She noticed the lights were on and saw someone moving around near the front counter. Steve appeared. He gave her a friendly wave and hustled to the door. "Good morning, Carlita."

"Hello, Steve."

Rambo trotted over to greet Autumn's brother.

"I talked to Autumn last night. She told me the cops arrested Sam Ivey for the death of his ex." Steve patted Rambo's head. "I saw the chick around here a couple of times."

Carlita perked up. "You did?"

"Yeah. In fact, she came in the shop last week asking about my prices, wanting to check out some of my work."

"How did she seem? I mean, was she strung out? Sane? Acting oddly?"

"She didn't strike me as being high or on drugs, if that's what you're asking." Steve told her he had no idea she was Sam's ex. "She never mentioned his name, only told me she was in town visiting a friend."

"Interesting," Carlita murmured. "Which means she's been around for a while."

"For sure. Autumn mentioned she was living in her car."

"We aren't certain, but believe it may have been the case." Carlita gave him a brief description of the vehicle.

"Gray convertible. I think I remember seeing it." Steve lit a cigarette and dropped the lighter in his front pocket. "She showed me one of her tats. Said she got it down in Miami. I kinda figured she was into drugs."

"How so?"

"Her tattoo. You got a minute?"

"Sure."

Steve finished his cigarette, ground it out in the ashtray by the door, and led the way inside. Carlita and Rambo followed him to the lounge area where he kept his tattoo books.

"Have a chair. It shouldn't take me long to find the tat." Steve flipped through a book and grabbed a second. "I know it's in here."

"What does it look like?"

"It's kinda hard to describe. There it is." He handed her the book.

"Which one?"

"The ribbon with the broken chain links."

Carlita studied the photo. The design was a ribbon that looped around. On the left-hand side of the loop were two chain links, broken and with jagged edges. "What does this have to do with drugs?"

"It's a recovery ribbon. You know, for people who are fighting or recovering from drug addiction."

"Natalie had one of these tattoos?"

"Yeah. It was a nice piece of work."

Carlita removed her cell phone from her pocket and took a picture of the tattoo. "What kind of tattoo was she interested in?"

Steve thought about it. "A butterfly. They're popular with women. She was thinking about putting it on her ankle."

"Is there anything else you remember about her?"

"No. I already talked to the cops. They were here yesterday, nosing around. I told them the same thing that I told you." Steve placed the books back on the table. "I don't know Sam as well as you do, but he doesn't strike me as the type to go around killing his ex."

"Unless she tried attacking him with her knife," Carlita said. "Regardless, I don't think Sam did it either. I think her killer was also her drug dealer. She owed him money."

Steve let out a low whistle. "Must've been a tidy chunk of change."

"Fifteen hundred bucks. At least, that's the amount she told Mercedes."

"Autumn said Mercedes is taking it pretty hard."

"It's been rough."

"I wish I could help."

"You and me both." Carlita thanked him for the information, and she and Rambo headed back out.

Had Natalie been living in her car, stalking Sam, waiting for the chance to beg him for more money? Mercedes mentioned Natalie had an upcoming modeling gig. It seemed like such a terrible waste of a young soul, a beautiful woman with so much promise and potential.

Carlita wondered about her family and parents. Did they know their daughter was dead? She couldn't imagine the pain of knowing your child's life had ended so needlessly, so violently.

She tried to shake the image of Natalie's last moments and slipped into the pawn shop. Tony and one of the employees were in the back, rearranging merchandise.

He caught his mother's eye and dropped what he was doing. "Hey, Ma. You're looking a little pale."

"I barely slept last night, worrying about Sam and Mercedes."

"It's a tough situation."

"Rambo and I ran into Steve on our way here." She filled her son in on their conversation. "It sounds like the woman had been hanging around for a while."

"Scoping out the territory," Tony said. "Reading between the lines, by the time she confronted Sam the other night, she was getting desperate."

"For good reason. Her killer was breathing down her neck." Carlita briefly closed her eyes.

"You're worried about Mercedes doing a little intel?"

"I am. Obviously, if those food truck employees are dealing drugs, they're going to be on guard."

"It stands to reason," he agreed. "On the other hand, if they're dealing drugs, it will be business as usual."

"I suppose."

The front bell rang, letting them know a customer had arrived.

Carlita trailed behind her son, following him out onto the store floor. "I gotta run next door and then head back to Pete's restaurant to meet with Elvira and her engineer."

"Let me know if I can help with the other."

She promised Tony she would and then backtracked through the rear employees-only entrance.

Carlita hesitated at the bottom of the stairs, wondering if she should check on Mercedes. Her daughter wasn't an early riser, not if she could help it.

Not wanting to wake her, she sent a text asking if she was okay. When she didn't reply, it confirmed what Carlita thought. Her daughter wasn't up yet.

She exited the building, making the quick trek to the restaurant. She greeted the prep staff, who were getting ready for the lunch crowd. Having already finished her inventory the previous day, she spent the next hour re-stocking the food truck while Rambo patiently stayed by her side.

She finished right on time and she and her pup hustled back home. They arrived to find Pete was already there. She caught up with him in his office at ten 'til ten. "I figured Elvira would already be here," she joked.

"Me too. Although she texted twice to remind me we were still on for ten o'clock," Pete said. "I told her to leave her demolition equipment at home."

Carlita grinned. "I bet she didn't like you setting down the rules."

"I reminded her it was my property and we would explore on my schedule, not hers."

"Good for you. You know Elvira. She'll railroad over the top of you to get what she wants."

"Which is why we'll have a thorough understanding about how this process will work from day one."

Carlita's cell phone chimed. "Speak of the devil. She and her engineer are near the hostess stand waiting for us."

Pete shoved his chair back and stood. "And on that note, let's get this show on the road."

Chapter 20

It wasn't hard to pick Elvira out of the group of people waiting to be seated in the lobby of the Parrot House Restaurant.

Perhaps it was because of her hair color—no longer gray, but more of a magenta shade. Or maybe it was her outfit—a 70s era black leather number with fringe running down both arms, from the armpits to slightly above the wrists. Tight black slacks and knee-high leather boots rounded out her ensemble.

Carlita said the first thing that popped into her head. "Where on earth did you get your outfit?"

"From a thrift store." Elvira twirled around. "Cool, huh?"

"It's...interesting." Carlita playfully tugged on a strand of purple hair. "What's this? Are you having a mid-life crisis?"

Elvira swatted her hand away, an annoyed look on her face. "I am not," she indignantly replied. "I'll have you know I've been invited to a biker chick's convention on Hutchinson Island. I'm heading over on the ferry after I leave here."

"Good. Which means you have no plans of knocking down my walls today," Pete said.

Elvira's eyes lit. "Was there a chance we could start whacking away at it? Because I'll gladly skip the chicks-on-bikes gathering if you wanna get cracking."

"No. There's no chance of exploration today. Other than to find out what your engineer has to say." Pete extended a hand. "You must be Stuart Wempley."

"Yes, sir." The tall, thin man coughed nervously. "Elvira said you were interested in having me look at your tunnel wall to give an opinion about the structural integrity."

"I am," Pete said. "I'm sure you're aware Elvira is itching to continue blowing tunnel walls out."

"Yes. I've been to her property several times. At my suggestion, more like warning, she's ceased demolition and put several projects on hold."

"For the time being," Elvira muttered under her breath. "I'm getting a second opinion."

"Which is certainly your right," the man replied. "However, I have warned against it."

Carlita's curiosity was piqued. "How structurally unsafe is Elvira's property?"

"I've suggested she add reinforcement beams." The engineer went into a long spiel about weight distribution, age of the structure, elements and materials used in the tunnel's construction.

Finally, Elvira cut him off. "We're not here to discuss my property. We're here to look at the tunnel below this restaurant."

Pete motioned for them to follow him. "It's down this way."

Wempley stopped him. "Elvira and I have an agreement. All of my inspections are prepaid."

"Prepaid?" Pete frowned. "I've never heard of prepaying. I can pay you as soon as you examine my tunnel."

"Unfortunately, Elvira and I have had a few...discrepancies which have resulted in me needing payment up front."

Carlita folded her arms, pinning her former tenant and neighbor with a stare. "Have you stiffed this guy?"

"She has a habit of short paying me," Wempley explained.

"We disagreed on the amount due," Elvira argued.

Pete rolled his eyes. "I don't have the time nor the inclination to stand here and discuss it all day. How much do you charge for a standard inspection?"

The engineer gave him an amount Carlita thought sounded fair. Pete told them to wait there. He left and returned moments later, check in hand.

Wempley held it up to the light to examine it.

"Let me guess...Elvira has written counterfeit checks," Carlita joked.

Elvira scowled. "I have no idea why Wempley is scrutinizing Pete's check."

"It looks good." The engineer pocketed the payment. "We can proceed."

Wempley followed Pete, while Elvira and Carlita trailed behind. They made their way down the center steps; the ones accessed via the main dining room.

Pete unlocked the door and escorted them through the tunnel. Wempley stopped when they reached the door with the metal bars, the one Elvira had successfully picked a few months back.

"What is it?" Carlita asked him.

"This door. Elvira and I were in this area."

Pete cleared his throat and stared at Elvira. "What were you doing over here?"

"Exploring," Elvira said. "I already told you I've been through most of these tunnels."

"You never stop," he sighed.

"Never," Carlita echoed.

"Let's keep moving."

They turned right and slowed their pace when the tunnel narrowed. Heavy, damp air became more prominent as they made their way toward the river.

"I have one more door to unlock." Pete made quick work of opening the heavy metal door. "We're getting close."

Finally, they reached the end. "We found some interesting carvings in this area. According to Elvira's depth-finding tool, we believe there might be a hollow spot behind this wall."

"Let's see what we have." Wempley shrugged his backpack off, unzipped the front, and began removing a set of small tools. Using a similar yet more sophisticated device than the one Elvira had used, he ran it along the wall...back and forth, from top to bottom.

Elvira nervously paced. "Well?"

"I'm still working." Wempley shot her an irritated glance. "It doesn't help with you pacing like a cat in a cage."

"I'll wait over there." Elvira scurried toward the other end. Using her cell phone's flashlight, she began examining the walls.

Finally, he finished with the depth gauge tool. He placed it back inside his backpack and removed what reminded Carlita of a miniature lawn mower. It had large wheels, a folding handle and a small flat screen resembling a solar panel. Wempley turned it on and began pushing it across the tunnel floor.

The device beeped, whirred, and hummed. Similar to testing the walls, the engineer ran it back and forth, back and forth.

Carlita grabbed Pete's arm and whispered in his ear. "Have you ever seen anything like that?"

"No. My structural guy did a visual check, poked around at a couple beams and left," he whispered back. "Mr. Wempley seems a lot more thorough."

Finally, the engineer finished his testing and joined them. "I'm almost done. I need to take a closer look at the overhead beams. They appear to be quite old."

Elvira must've been eavesdropping because she made a mad dash over. "It's not any older than my tunnel."

"The tunnels are all around the same age," Wempley agreed. "My concern now would be the age of the ceiling structure. These beams are even older than the ones in your building."

"They are," Pete confirmed. "My restaurant is 250 years old, one of the oldest standing structures in Georgia."

"And a piece of history," Wempley added. "Which is why I intend to handle this project with utmost care."

Elvira placed her hands on the sides of her forehead, a pained expression on her face. "You're killing me here. I can already see where this is headed."

"I appreciate Mr. Wempley's thorough examination," Pete said. "The last thing I want is to rip a hole in the wall and have my business crash down around my ears—literally."

Elvira ignored Pete's comment. "How much longer?"

"Not much," Wempley said. "I would like to examine the beams, but need a ladder."

"Use your flashlight," Elvira said. "You don't need to get up close."

"Elvira Cobb," Carlita scolded. "Stop badgering him."

Wempley adjusted his glasses. "I'm accustomed to Elvira's pressure tactics. They don't work."

"I'll go grab a ladder." Pete left. He reappeared in record time, ladder in hand. "This should do the trick."

"Thank you." The engineer unfolded it and climbed to the top.

He pulled a flashlight from his pocket and aimed it at the beams. "The workmanship is outstanding. This structure could easily last another century."

"Wonderful," Pete said. "I hope it does."

Wempley climbed back down and dusted his hands. "What exactly are your plans for this tunnel?"

"Based on some drawings we found and the fact both you and Elvira agree there may be a sizable hollow spot behind this tunnel wall, we were thinking about perhaps doing some exploration. We would start by removing a small section to see what may be behind it."

"Perhaps?" Elvira's jaw dropped. "No siree. We are definitely doing some exploring. It's not a matter of if, but when."

Pete glared at her. "Your treasure-hunting brain is clouding your thought process. Must I remind you this is my property, my tunnel, and *if* I decide to chip away at the wall, it will be my project?"

Elvira defiantly met Pete's scowl. For a brief second, Carlita thought her husband was going to throw her out. He relaxed his stance—slightly. "Understood?"

"Yes," she said in a small voice. "I'm just excited. We're onto something here. I can feel it in my bones."

"I believe we may be onto something as well. But again, I will not explore until I'm certain the building is structurally safe and sound."

"When you say explore, are we talking about taking a brick or two out or removing a larger section?" the engineer asked.

Elvira made an unhappy sound. "Why does it matter?"

"It matters because we don't want Pete's restaurant to end up in the same condition as your basement," Carlita said. "With holes in the walls and piles of rubble from being blown up."

"It wasn't my fault," Elvira interrupted. "Those clowns Damon and Jamie were the ones who set the explosives."

"The last time," Pete reminded her.

"Let's not nitpick over minor details," Elvira said.

Pete motioned to the engineer. "If I move forward with this project, my plan would be to remove a small section of the wall to see what's on the other side. Depending on what we find, we might need to remove a little more."

"I think we're going to have to remove a lot more," Elvira said.

"Stop." Pete made a timeout with his hands. "Stop talking."

Carlita grasped Elvira's arm and propelled her away from Pete. "You're not helping."

Elvira pursed her lips, a sullen look on her face.

"To answer your question, only a small hole to start," Pete said.

"I see." Wempley went into a long technical explanation again about materials, structures, weight distribution, and even threw in a concern about the proximity to the river.

"In other words, being this close to the Savannah River is somewhat of a concern," Pete summarized.

"Correct. Because of the proximity to the river, my suggestion is to add three support posts. One at each end of the tunnel and a third in the center."

"How long would this take?" Pete asked. "Ballpark estimate."

"A couple of weeks. The posts would need to be ordered. Installing them isn't difficult. You put them in place, make sure they're level, ratchet them up and you're good to go." The engineer rattled off a rough estimate. "You don't have to give me an answer right now if you would like to take some time to think about it."

"Time is money," Elvira said.

Carlita wagged her finger at her.

"We can't give up now."

Wempley held up his hand. "I have one other suggestion. You could drill a hole and attach a camera or some other small recording device to it to see what you can find."

"No way." Elvira shook her head. "I can tell you from experience you need a larger hole to see anything. It would be a waste of time."

"Elvira would know." Carlita chuckled. "She's the expert."

Pete shot his wife a quick look. He crouched down to examine one of the carvings. And Carlita could see he was torn. On the one hand, what if something was behind the wall?

On the other hand, whatever was behind the wall had been there for a very long time. Perhaps even hundreds of years. She thought about the saying, "Some things are better left alone."

Pete slowly stood. "I've heard rumors about a lost pirate ship, lost treasure. The story has persisted for decades. It started circulating long before I was ever born. Before my father was ever born. To his dying day, Dad insisted a pirate ship was somewhere around here, lost during a catastrophic hurricane."

He turned to his wife. "This is your home now. Whatever I decide will affect you as well. What do you think?"

Carlita studied his face. She could see a spark of something. The Parrot House Restaurant was a piece of history. A piece of Savannah's history. A piece of her husband's history. At the end of the day, it was his decision.

"This is all up to you, Pirate Pete Taylor. This is your story to tell. If you want to see what's behind this wall, I'm with you one hundred percent. If you decide to let the pirate lore and legend live on, I'm also on board."

Elvira crept closer, licking her lips, waiting for Pete to answer.

He pressed the palm of his hand on the brick, thoughtfully contemplating the wall which had stood the test of time, survived wars, hurricanes, death and destruction. "I don't need to think about it. I've made my decision."

Chapter 21

"I'm going to let whatever is behind this wall rest in peace," Pete finally said.

Elvira clutched her throat and dropped to her knees. "You're kidding," she gasped. "We're so close...so close to finding something. All my hard work, the money I've spent, not to mention time and energy, and you're going to throw it all away."

Carlita, noting how clearly upset Elvira was at the thought she wasn't going to find out what was behind Pete's tunnel wall, patted her arm. "Maybe Pete's right. It's better left alone. Tampering with the wall might open a can of worms."

Seemingly not hearing Carlita's reasoning, the distraught woman flopped over. Flat on her back, she stared up at the ceiling.

"We might have to carry her out of here," Pete joked.

"This isn't the end of the world." Carlita tugged on Elvira's hand, trying to pull her up off the ground. "You can still search for treasure. Maybe you should focus your efforts on the water."

"I've already done some preliminary investigating. I thought I was onto something when Sharky was here. It turned out to be a big fat nothing. I've wasted a lot of time and energy."

Pete stepped away from the group, slowly making his way to the end of the tunnel, an unreadable expression on his face, and Carlita could see an internal battle was waging.

She left Elvira to wallow in her misery and quietly crept in behind him.

He must've felt her presence because he spun around. "Do you think I'm making a mistake?"

Carlita carefully chose her words. "No. I'm not sure what I would do if I were in your shoes. On one hand, I would always wonder what might be behind the wall. Of course, there's always the option of changing your mind."

"True." Pete glanced over Carlita's shoulder at Elvira, who was still on the ground, her eyes closed. "She's really depressed about my decision."

"Because she's spent the last few years sleeping, eating, breathing, basically obsessed with finding treasure," Carlita said. "Maybe you're saving her from deep disappointment."

"Despite her being one of the most annoying people I've ever met, she's helped us out."

"Multiple times."

"Even now, with Mercedes."

"Yes."

Pete lowered his voice. "I'm having second thoughts."

"Your decision shouldn't be based on Elvira's reaction."

"I know." He ran a light hand over the bricks. "As I stood here, I could almost hear my father's voice, telling me to go for it."

"To see what is behind here?"

"Yes."

Stuart Wempley finished packing up his gear and made his way over. "I'll give you another one of my cards in case you decide sometime down the road to move forward with the project."

"It won't be necessary. I've changed my mind. I would like to install the support posts."

Elvira scrambled to her feet. She shoved Wempley out of the way and threw herself at Pete, wrapping her arms around his neck as she jumped up and down. "You had me going for a minute, Taylor. I thought you were serious."

"I *was* serious."

"You won't regret this." Elvira finally released her death grip, much to Pete's relief. "I know this might be a tricky project, so I'll be doing my due diligence."

"This is still my property—my project," Pete reminded her.

"Yes, siree." Elvira gave him a snappy salute. "I can't believe it. This is the best day ever."

"We haven't done anything yet."

"But we're on our way." Elvira jabbed her finger at the engineer. "Don't drag your feet. You need to get those support posts ordered ASAP."

Wempley rubbed his thumb and fingers together. "Money. I need a deposit to pay for the posts."

"I'll write you another check." Pete brought up the rear, locking the door behind them. They reached the main passageway and he lingered, gazing back toward the area they'd left.

Carlita could only imagine what he was thinking. Would they find something? Or was he spending money on a project which would turn out to be nothing? Only time would tell.

After making the payment, Elvira and her engineer left first. Pete wasn't far behind, claiming he had a staff meeting on board The Flying Gunner.

With time to kill, Carlita ran upstairs, grabbed Rambo, and meandered up and down the city blocks. She discovered the Book Nook was open and lingered on the sidewalk near the front picture window, noticing a book which looked vaguely familiar.

It was one of Mercedes' most recent novels, *True Crime Mafia. Life in the Family.* Curious to find out if her daughter's books were selling, she wandered inside.

Cricket Tidwell, the bookstore owner, stood in the back waiting on a customer. She completed the transaction, and the man left. "Good morning, Carlita."

"Good morning, Cricket. Rambo and I were walking past and noticed Mercedes' mafia book in your front window."

"I rotate local authors' books. It was Mercedes' turn to take the spotlight." Cricket clasped her hands. "It's selling well. I had no idea readers were interested in mafia families. I read the book myself and was impressed by the amount of research Mercedes must have put into writing it."

"You have no idea," Carlita said. "I'm hoping she eventually branches out and writes something different."

"Like what?"

"Romance. Cozy mysteries, something a little less violent."

"Speaking of violent, I heard about the poor woman who was murdered a couple blocks from here."

"Natalie Lameron," Carlita said.

"A customer mentioned the police have made an arrest."

"They arrested my tenant, Sam Ivey."

Cricket's jaw dropped. "Mercedes' boyfriend, the former cop?"

"Yeah. I don't think he killed her. From what I understand, she had a drug problem and owed her dealer money."

The bookstore owner shook her head. "Such a sad situation. Hopefully, the police will sort it out. How is Mercedes holding up?"

"Better than I thought." Carlita patted her pockets. "I would like to buy Mercedes' book. Do you take Apple Pay?"

"Apple-solutely," Cricket joked. "Would you like a paperback or hardcover copy?"

"I'll go grab a hardcover." Carlita ran to the front of the store, grabbed a copy of Mercedes' book from the stack, and carried it to the counter. She rarely used the mobile payment service, so it took a minute for her to figure it out.

The transaction went through and Cricket handed her the bagged book. "Mercedes will be thrilled to know we've sold a few of her books this week."

"Every penny counts." Carlita carried her bag from the store and she and Rambo continued their stroll through the neighborhood, taking a different route this time.
They found themselves in front of the Thirsty Crow, smack dab in the center of City Market.

They started to stroll past when she glimpsed her tenant, Cool Bones, near the bar's stage. She stuck her head in the door and gave him a quick wave.

Cool Bones waved back and then motioned for her to wait.

He hurried to the door. "Hello, Carlita, Rambo."

Rambo nudged Cool Bones' hand. "I sure do miss seeing you guys walking around the neighborhood."

"We miss it too, although it's nice having Morrell Park even closer. It's Rambo's favorite spot."

"I was home last night when the cops came by. Is Sam still..."

"In jail? As far as I know," Carlita said. "I haven't talked to Mercedes yet today. She's not an early riser, so I figured with everything going on, she might be sleeping in. We're working at the food truck this afternoon."

"At the risk of not minding my own business, what happened?" Cool Bones asked. "I know it involved some woman who was found dead a couple of nights ago."

"The woman was Sam's ex."

Cool Bones blinked rapidly. "Sam's ex?"

"It's a long story and involves drugs."

He let out a low whistle. "Not good."

"Not at all."

They made small talk for a few more minutes until it was time for Carlita to drop her pup off at home and head back over to meet with Mercedes.

She was halfway there when her daughter finally replied to the earlier text. Her heart sank when she read what it said. *The cops just left.*

Chapter 22

Carlita promptly texted her daughter back. *Do you want me to find someone to cover your shift at the food truck?*

No. I'll meet you in the alley in less than five.

I need to drop Rambo off at home first. I'll be there as soon as I can, Carlita texted back.

Mercedes beat her time and was waiting, or more like pacing, in the alley when Carlita arrived. "That was fast."

"I was already ready when the cops swung by to ask a bunch of questions."

"About Sam," Carlita guessed.

"Sam and Natalie. They wanted to know if I knew someone named Peyton Price."

"Who is Peyton Price?"

"A local. The cops found his number programmed in Natalie's phone. I guess it was a friend of hers and she'd been staying with him."

"So, she wasn't living in her car."

"Not all the time. Reading between the lines, she was crashing on his couch."

"Maybe he was the one who killed her," Carlita said.

"I was thinking the same thing. In fact, I was gonna do a little digging around, but didn't have time." Mercedes absentmindedly patted her pocket. "Good. I didn't forget my cell phone. I was in such a hurry to get out the door, I thought for a minute I forgot it."

"I wonder how Sam is holding up."

"He's okay. I talked to him last night and this morning."

"He got more than the one obligatory allotted call?" her mother asked.

"Sam's got several friends who still work at the station, so he's getting some extra perks." Mercedes told her mother she was hoping the judge would set bail. "I offered to post bail once he knew for sure. I feel terrible."

"Why? Because you got caught in the middle of his mess, he's in jail, and you feel guilty because you took the break he suggested you two take?"

"Now that you put it like that," Mercedes said. "Poor Sadie moped around all morning. She misses Sam and so do I."

"You're having second thoughts about the break."

"Yeah. I mean, I know Sam didn't kill Natalie. I've been trying to see his side of it and, to be honest, I believe he was trying to protect me from her."

Carlita slipped her arm through her daughter's on their way to the end of the alley. "He's lucky to have you. You're as loyal as they come."

"Loyal or looney," Mercedes quipped. "The jury is still out."

"Do you still want to try buying drugs from you-know-who?"

"Yes, even though it could be a dead end. All I know is the cops have another suspect—Natalie's friend."

"Which could be good news."

Mercedes changed the subject. "How did it go with Elvira, her engineer, and the tunnel inspection?"

"The guy told Pete if he wants to tear into the wall, he needs to add some support posts. At first, he was against it. He was going to leave it as is."

"Let the past remain dead and buried," Mercedes said. "I bet Elvira flipped out."

"Close. She had a major meltdown."

"Elvira changed Pete's mind?"

"No. I think curiosity won out."

Mercedes rubbed her palms together. "Look at everything we've found since we've been here? For all we know, our gems could have been the tip of the iceberg."

"It's a thought."

They reached the restaurant's rear entrance. Mercedes waited in the alley while Carlita ran inside to grab the food truck's keys. She stepped back out and tossed them to her daughter before climbing in.

Reaching the entrance to Freedom Square, they discovered a crowd of people had already gathered near the gates. Mercedes slowed, dodging several pedestrians on the way to their designated spot.

"Can you believe how busy this place is for a Monday?"

"I never knew an art festival could be so popular." Mercedes backed the food truck in between a pair of towering live oaks and shut the engine off. "I figured we would handle the lunch crunch and then I would try to make a purchase next door to see what happens."

"Sounds like a plan."

The main gates opened moments later. Mother and daughter hit the ground running. Business was brisk. They worked seamlessly together, filling containers with delicious Italian dishes, thick slices of buttery garlic bread, and fresh salads. Arnie had even added a tray of crispy, creamy cannoli.

It was music to Carlita's ears every time the cash register rang. It meant each new customer who tried, tasted and loved their authentic Italian dishes might stop by Ravello's for a sit-down dinner.

Finally, the crowd thinned. Luigi appeared and waited off to the side until they finished helping a customer.

"Hey, Mrs. GT, Mercedes. Have you heard from Sam?"

"He's hoping the judge will post bail. As soon as he does, I'm gonna run over and drop off the cash."

"You guys back together?"

"Not yet," Mercedes said. "The cops stopped by my place earlier."

Luigi arched a brow. "To ask you about Sam?"

"Sam and someone named Peyton Price. He's a local and was a friend of Natalie's."

"Is he the drug dealer?"

"I don't know." Mercedes lowered her voice. "I'm still doing a little intel. There's a lull in business. It shouldn't be picking back up for at least another half hour."

"You're thinking about making a purchase soon?" Luigi asked.

"Yeah."

"Cool. I'll hang around to keep an eye out."

"Thank you, Luigi. I'll feel much better knowing you're nearby." Carlita grabbed a clean spatula. "You look hungry. What would you like for lunch?"

"You don't have to feed me."

"I know I don't *have* to. I want to." She waved the spatula in the air. "If you don't tell me, I'll pick."

"I've been thinkin' about your deep dish lasagna, how it makes my mouth water."

"Lasagna it is." Carlita eased two large slices into a container. She grabbed a second empty container and added garlic bread. Before closing the lid, she squeezed in a cannoli. She placed the containers on the counter, reached for an Italian soda, and set it next to the food.

"I could die a happy man right now," Luigi joked.

"I hope not." Carlita plucked a set of disposable dinnerware from the tray and handed it to him. "Bon appétit."

"Bon appétit sounds better than over the lips, past the gums, look out stomach, here it comes," he joked.

"Either way, enjoy."

"I'll be nearby, keeping an eye out." Luigi rambled off. He settled on an empty bench, giving him a bird's-eye view of Ravello's food truck as well as the Candy Cart.

"I guess it's now or never." Mercedes untied her apron and lifted it over her head.

"You want me to try making the buy?" Carlita asked.

Her daughter wrinkled her nose. "You go over and try to score a bag of drugs?"

"Yeah. I mean, I'm sure people my age buy dope all the time."

"Drugs don't discriminate. Having said that, you don't fit the profile."

"Neither do you," Carlita said.

"What do you plan to say?"

"You got any green stuff for sale?"

Mercedes burst out laughing. "Green stuff for sale?"

"I don't know." Her mother shrugged. "I've never bought drugs before. I would find a more appropriate line first."

"You would be buying a bag," Mercedes said. "A bag is slang for marijuana."

"Okay. I would say. How much is a bag?"

"What kind of bag?"

"Medium size."

Mercedes clamped a hand over her mouth and shook her head.

"No? There's no such thing as a medium bag?"

"You would ask for deluxe, primo or an economy bag," Mercedes said. "I plan to price all three."

Carlita clutched her throat. "The thought of it is giving me hives."

"Which is why I'm the one who is going to see if they're running a side business." Mercedes hung her apron on the hook. "Wish me luck."

"You got this." Carlita held the door, watching as Mercedes circled around behind the food truck and came out on the other side. With determined steps, she marched across the square and walked right up to the window.

Why am I getting such a bad feeling about this? Carlita clenched her fists, barely able to breathe as her daughter approached the window. *Keep an eye out for her, Luigi. Something about this doesn't feel right.*

Chapter 23

Beads of sweat formed on Mercedes' brow. An equal amount of sweat made her armpits wet and sticky as she approached the Candy Cart food truck's counter.

She lingered a few feet away, waiting for the guy in front of her to place his order. "Yeah. I'll take a premium bag of swirl pops. I have seventy-five bucks."

"Seventy-five will buy you a nice bag of candy, enough to last a couple days." The man reached into the cabinet and removed a brown paper bag. "I'm running out of change, so I would appreciate it if you had the exact amount."

The customer dug into his jeans pocket, pulled out a handful of crumpled bills and set them on the counter. "Thanks, man. How long are you open today?"

"Until the festival closes."

"I might be back." He tucked the bag in his jacket pocket and moseyed off.

Mercedes approached the counter. "Hello."

"Hello."

"I would like to place an order...for a...bag," she stammered.

"A bag." The man leaned in, eyeing her curiously. "A bag of caramel corn or cotton candy? We also have some bags of freeze-dried space candy."

"Space candy?"

"Skittles, Lemonheads, gummy sharks." He tilted his head. "You work over at the Italian food truck."

"I do."

"I thought you looked familiar. Your manicotti is the bomb."

"Thanks."

"You're welcome. So, what did you want to order?"

"I was thinking more along the lines of 520." As soon as Mercedes said it, she knew she'd flubbed up. *420 dummy. The slang for marijuana is 420.*

The employee behind the counter scratched his head. "I don't know what you're talking about. Do you want to buy some candy or not? Customers are waiting behind you."

Mercedes glanced over her shoulder. He was right. Others were in line, ready to place orders. "I'll have to pass." She hurriedly walked away, going in the opposite direction of the food truck.

Her scalp tingled, and she was almost certain the employee was watching her. Mercedes stopped at the nearest trash can, pretended to drop something inside and then casually walked back to Ravello's food truck.

"Well?" Carlita asked as soon as she stepped inside. "How did it go?"

Mercedes gave her a thumbs down. "It was a bust."

"They aren't selling drugs?"

"No. I think they're selling drugs. They just didn't want to sell them to me." Mercedes blew air through thinned lips. "I screwed up. Instead of telling them I wanted 420, code word for marijuana, I told him I wanted a 520."

"What is 520?"

"Good question."

Carlita grabbed her phone and typed 520 in the search bar. She burst out laughing.

"What does it mean?"

"It means love."

Mercedes' eyes widened in horror. "I told the guy I wanted love?"

"It appears so."

"Great. He probably thinks I'm some sort of weirdo." Mercedes told her mother about the young guy ahead of her who bought a brown bag. "He said he had seventy-five bucks for a premium bag of swirl pops."

"Maybe premium bag was the key phrase," Carlita guessed.

"It worked a lot better than telling him I wanted a 520."

"At least you tried."

"But we're not any closer to figuring out for sure if the Candy Cart is selling drugs. We need someone more legit to try to score a sale."

"Luigi is out," Carlita said.

"So is Tony, especially if Natalie's drug dealer was the one he caught on camera inside the pawn shop the other day."

"Pete could try to buy drugs."

Mercedes immediately shot down the idea. "Pete's face is everywhere. He's easily recognizable by most people who live in the area."

"I bet Steve Winter could buy and seem legit."

Luigi reappeared. "The food was delish. Thanks again." He nodded to Mercedes. "How did it go?"

"I blew it. I told the guy I wanted a 520."

"What's a 520?"

"Love," Mercedes said. "The guy behind the counter probably thinks I'm some sort of fruitcake. So, we're not any closer to figuring out if the Candy Cart is selling drugs."

"No offense, but if they are running a side business, you don't fit the description of their clientele."

"Exactly. You're out. Ma and Pete are out. Tony won't work. Dernice and Elvira have been all over this place, working. We're running out of ideas."

"I might have something in mind," Luigi said. "Give me a little time to see what I can come up with."

Mercedes brightened. "Seriously? That would be awesome."

"Don't get your hopes up. I'll keep you posted."

Carlita waited until Luigi walked away. "While you were gone, I did a little research to see if I could find anything out about Natalie's friend Peyton Price."

"And?"

"He owns a house nearby. Actually, from what I can tell, it looks like some sort of duplex or triplex."

"Maybe we can swing by and take a quick look around after we're done here," Mercedes said.

"I was thinkin' the same thing." Carlita took care of a customer and waited until he walked away. "Any word from Sam?"

"Not a peep. Maybe the judge isn't going to post bail after all."

"Could be. We'll have to worry about it later. It looks like we're about to get slammed."

The afternoon hours flew by. If anything, their food truck was as busy as it had been over the weekend. By the time three-thirty rolled around, they were running low on several dishes.

At four on the dot, Carlita rolled the overhead door down and snapped the lock in place. "Another day in the books."

"I don't know about you, but my feet are killing me," Mercedes groaned.

"Ditto. I think I'm going to go home and soak in a nice hot bath."

"Me too." Mercedes slipped her shoes off and limped over to the sink, finishing the last of the cleanup so they could hit the road. "We don't have to swing by Peyton Price's place if you're too tired."

"Nah. It's right around the corner. You drive and I'll direct," Carlita said.

"It's a deal." Mercedes made sure the cabinets were secured before taking her place behind the wheel. They ran into a minor backup. Other vendors were heading out, which meant a slight delay in exiting Freedom Square.

Turning left, they crisscrossed several narrow side streets before reaching an area of town Carlita had visited many times. In fact, it wasn't far from Walton Square.

Mercedes turned onto another street and tapped the brakes. "This place is close to home."

"I was thinking the same thing. In fact, these buildings remind me of ours. I'm sure they were built around the same time."

The road narrowed, forcing Mercedes to swing wide to make it around the corner.

They crept along at a snail's pace, barely squeezing past the parked vehicles.

"Yikes. This is a tight fit." Mercedes grimaced as the driver's side mirror cleared a parked van's mirror by mere inches. "Note to self. Don't bring the food truck down these narrow side streets."

"We're almost there." Carlita consulted the map on her phone. They had almost reached their destination.

Mercedes slammed on the brakes.

Carlita's head snapped back. "Careful."

"Sorry, Ma. A cat ran out in front of me." She craned her neck, making sure the orange tabby was safely out of the way. "Tell me we're close."

"We're close." Carlita tapped the screen. "It's directly ahead, on the right."

They crept forward a few more feet.

Carlita rolled the window down to take a closer look. "Hey, Mercedes. Are you seeing what I'm seeing?"

Chapter 24

"This is definitely Peyton Price's place," Mercedes said excitedly. "Are you thinking what I'm thinking?"

"I hope not." Carlita stared at the rainbow-colored parasail plastered on the side of the van. Splashed above it, in bright blue letters, was "Peyton's Parasailing." Listed below the parasail was a local phone number.

"We need to figure out how close he and Natalie were."

"Agreed. I mean, if she was in contact with him recently, he could be her killer," Carlita said.

"Or at the very least he might have some information about who her drug dealer was," Mercedes said. "She said 'he', which means it could be Peyton Price."

"Would he be dumb enough to kill her, knowing she had called him prior to her death?" Carlita asked. "I don't think anyone would be that stupid."

"We need to delve a little deeper into their relationship."

"How do you propose we do that?"

"By becoming a customer."

"I was afraid you were gonna suggest something along those lines," Carlita sighed. "I don't know how I feel about you parasailing. Those things can cut loose and fall from the sky or crash into high rises."

Mercedes half-listened to her mother as she fiddled with her phone.

"What are you doing?"

"Finding out where they're located. I have some good news. It's based out of Tybee Island."

"Why is this good news?"

"Because Tybee doesn't have high rises," Mercedes said.

"Mercedes Garlucci, yes they do."

"But not skyscraper tall," her daughter insisted.

"What about the lighthouse?"

"Our chances of having some sort of freak accident and hitting the lighthouse are next to nil."

Carlita made a timeout. "Did you just say *our* chances?"

"Yeah. You and me."

"Parasailing?" Carlita clutched her gut. "I'm gettin' queasy just thinkin' about it."

"I could ask Autumn to go with me."

"Yeah." Carlita warmed to the idea. "Autumn and you can parasail. I'll stand on shore and watch. I'll even pay for it."

"Let me give her a quick call." Mercedes dialed her friend's cell phone number.

"Hey, Mercedes."

"Hey, Autumn."

"I was just thinking about you. Is Sam out of jail?"

"Not yet. At least, he hasn't asked me to post bond."

"One of my colleagues has been following the story. I guess the cops have someone else on their radar."

"Peyton Price. He's the reason I'm calling. I have you on speaker. Ma is with me."

"Hey, Mrs. G."

"Hello, Autumn."

Mercedes briefly filled her in. "We're parked across the street from his place. He owns a parasailing business."

"Parasailing. I've always wanted to try it," Autumn said.

"Awesome. You might be in luck. I was thinking about doing a little detective work and figured I would take a parasailing excursion with Peyton. Do you want to come with me?"

"I would love to. Unfortunately, I can't. Remember when I tripped and fell last winter outside the apartment and ended up with a concussion?"

"Yeah."

"I can't do any kind of jarring activities. Parasailing, rollercoasters, anything which could potentially knock my noggin around, at least for a few more months."

"Crud."

"It's a bummer," Autumn said. "What about Shelby?"

"She's pregnant. I don't think she's up for it."

"Tony?"

"I love my brother. But he's a practical joker. I can envision him trying to scare the crap out of me."

"True. What about you, Mrs. G?"

"I'm not sure parasailing is something I want to try." Carlita tugged on her seatbelt. "Being tethered to a rope with nothing between me and the open water, not to mention putting my life in the hands of a complete stranger, makes me feel a little sick."

"I wish I had a better idea. Luigi might work." Autumn immediately dismissed him. "I think they have some sort of weight restriction. He's a big guy."

Carlita and Mercedes thanked her for the ideas before her daughter said goodbye. "We're at a standstill."

"For the time being. Why don't you check on Sam?" Carlita suggested.

"Good idea." Mercedes dialed his number. The call went directly to voicemail. "Hey Sam. It's Mercedes. Call me when you get this message."

"Elvira might be able to find out Sam's status." Carlita slid her phone from her purse and noticed someone had left a voicemail message. She entered her pin number and pressed the play button.

"Hello, Mrs. Taylor. Attorney Watson here. I've obtained a copy of the police report if you would like to swing by my office to pick it up." He rattled off his address before ending the call.

"While we're out, we might as well stop by and grab the report." Mercedes snapped a picture of Peyton's parasailing van before driving off. "I'm not giving up on finding out how close Natalie and Peyton Price were."

"I figured as much." Carlita entered the attorney's office address and directed her daughter through the side streets. They reached a more upscale downtown area, one Carlita rarely visited.

"This is his building." She craned her neck, peering through a set of gold and glass doors at expensive-looking marble floors. "No wonder Watson's prices are outrageous. He has to pay for this swanky office."

Mercedes eased the food truck into an empty parking spot and shifted into park. "You want me to go in with you?"

"No." Carlita reached for the door handle. "With the prices he charges, I can't afford to stay long. It should only take a minute." She hurried inside, her sneakers squeak-squeaking with each step she took.

Discovering the lobby's reception desk was empty, Carlita stepped over to the bank of elevators and began searching the list for Buster Watson's floor.

"Five ten." Carlita jabbed the "up" button. The elevator doors opened to an equally ornate interior. She stepped inside and hit the button for the floor she needed.

The elevator doors shut and began moving in slow motion. Two...three...four... There was a dull grinding sound. The elevator shuddered. The lights flickered right before they went out, leaving Carlita in the dark.

Chapter 25

Carlita fought the feeling of claustrophobia that was starting to kick in. She grabbed her cell phone and turned the flashlight on.

Aiming it at the panel of buttons, she pressed the button for the fifth floor again. Nothing happened. She pressed the door open, the door closed, and then the "call for help" button.

Again, nothing.

"Great. I'm stuck in an elevator." An elevated sense of panic set in when she realized she had no cell service. *Stay calm. You'll eventually get out.*

Thinking she might be close enough to the next floor for someone to hear her, she started banging on the doors. "Help! I'm stuck in the elevator. Help! Can anyone hear me?"

Carlita pressed the buttons again. Up. Down. Door open. Door closed. The help button. She pressed one with a bell symbol, all to no avail.

Surely, someone would realize the elevator wasn't moving. Mercedes would wonder what had happened to her mother and come looking for her.

Carlita kept her finger on the open door button and began hollering. "If you can hear me, I'm stuck in the elevator between the fourth and fifth floor!"

She continued pressing and calling for help. She checked her phone and found she'd been trapped in the elevator for six minutes.

Hold tight. No need to panic. You'll be out soon. Despite knowing her situation wouldn't last much longer, Carlita struggled to remain calm. What if the elevator malfunctioned and it crashed to the ground?

Stop, she silently scolded herself. *You're going to be fine.*

Her heart raced. What if no one realized the elevator was stuck? She tapped the floor button again. It made a grinding sound, followed by a whirring. The lights flickered and came on.

Seconds later, the doors opened on the fifth floor. A small crowd stood gathered in front, waiting to go down. "The elevator got stuck on the way up."

"Old Ellie got you," a woman said. "She gets stuck once or twice a week."

Carlita blinked rapidly. "This happens often?"

"Like clockwork," a man said. "The key is to press and hold the help button. The maintenance staff is notified and they'll reset the switches."

"Thanks for the warning. I think I'll take the stairs back down." Carlita greeted the woman at the receptionist's desk, telling her who she was. "Attorney Watson said he had a copy of a report for me."

"I have it right here." The woman placed a large brown envelope with her name neatly printed across the front on the counter.

Carlita reached for it and hesitated. "Am I gonna be billed for taking this?"

"No. Before Attorney Watson left for a meeting, he dropped this off and said you might be picking it up."

She eyed the woman suspiciously. "You're sure I'm not gonna be billed for taking this?"

"Almost one hundred percent."

Carlita tucked the envelope under her arm. "Can you tell me how to find the stairs?"

"Over there." The receptionist pointed to a door on the right with an "Emergency Exit" sign overhead.

"Thank you." She entered the stairwell, making her way down the steps until she reached the main floor.

Carlita crossed the lobby, nodding to a man who now stood behind the counter. "I could've used him about fifteen minutes ago," she muttered under her breath.

Reaching the sidewalk, she hopped back in the food truck and found her daughter talking on her cell phone. "Who are you..."

Mercedes pressed a finger to her lips. "I see. Half off the second person is tempting. You said you have an opening tomorrow morning at nine? Pencil us in, party of two."

Mercedes grew quiet. "You need a name. Put the reservation under Carlita Taylor. I have a card for the reservation fee."

Carlita began shaking her head.

"It will be a Visa card." Mercedes snapped her fingers and motioned to her mother's purse.

"This is nuts." Carlita reluctantly removed her wallet. She handed Mercedes her credit card.

"I have the number. Whenever you're ready." Mercedes read her mother's credit card number and handed it back. "I have until six this evening to cancel and get a full refund?" She thanked the person, ended the call, and triumphantly waved the phone in the air. "We're all set."

"I thought I made it clear I wasn't on board to go parasailing."

Mercedes waved a discount travel book in the air. "I found this travel book in one of those sidewalk boxes. I began flipping through it and saw Peyton's Parasailing offering a discount—half off the second person. I couldn't resist. Besides, the guy on the phone, I'm pretty sure it was Peyton, promised it would be a smooth ride."

Carlita snapped her seatbelt in place, grumbling under her breath.

"I thought I lost you," Mercedes said. "Did you get my text?"

"No. I was stuck in the elevator."

Her daughter made a choking sound. "Just now?"

"Yeah, between the fourth and fifth floor. I could've been stuck for hours."

"No way. As soon as I was done booking the parasailing, I was gonna come look for you," Mercedes said. "Did you get the report?"

"Yeah." Carlita set her purse on the floor. "I figured we could take a look at it when we get back to your place."

It was a short drive to Walton Square, where Arnie, the manager, was on hand to help them unload. "How did it go?"

"It was busier than I thought it would be," Carlita said. "We were handing out flyers left and right. Have you noticed an uptick in business these past few days?"

"As a matter of fact, I have."

While Arnie, Mercedes and an employee unloaded the truck, Carlita ran inside to empty the cash register. She went over the receipts and caught up with the others who were finishing up.

"I was telling Mercedes, I got a couple employees who are interested in running the food truck tomorrow if you would like a day off."

"And I told Arnie it would work out perfectly, seeing how we have plans first thing tomorrow morning," Mercedes said.

"Plans. How could I forget?" Carlita sucked in a breath.

"Something good?" the manager asked.

"Yes," Mercedes said.

"No," Carlita answered at the same time.

He chuckled. "I got a yes and a no. Which is it?"

"Mercedes has us booked to go parasailing on Tybee Island."

Arnie laughed. "You're going parasailing?"

"Maybe. I reserve the right to change my mind."

Mercedes flung her arm across her mother's shoulder. "But you won't."

"Probably not. I'm not sure how safe it is."

"My son went parasailing out on Tybee. He had a blast," Arnie said.

"How old is your son?"

"About Mercedes' age."

"I rest my case. I'm too old for high-flying adventures."

"You are not." Mercedes playfully nudged her. "You're one of the most adventurous people I know."

"Have fun." Arnie told them not to worry about the truck. He would make sure it was loaded, set up, and ready to roll.

"You're a doll," Carlita said. "Have I ever told you that you're the best restaurant manager I've ever had?"

"No, but I suppose this would be true, considering I'm the only restaurant manager you've ever had."

"It makes no difference. You're the best." Carlita thanked him and told him to call if he needed anything before she and Mercedes trekked along the alley to the apartment.

Elvira's security services van roared down the alley, screeching to a halt within feet of where mother and daughter stood. The driver's side window lowered.

Elvira leaned her elbow out the open window. "I got some bad news."

"What sort of bad news?" Carlita asked.

"Stuart said the support posts are on back order. He's not sure when they're coming in."

"I'll let Pete know. I don't think it will be a problem. He's in no hurry."

"I am. I don't want to give Pete time to change his mind again."

"He's not going to change his mind," Carlita said. "He told you he would move forward with the project and he will."

"You're sure?"

"One hundred percent."

Elvira changed the subject. "Have you heard from Sam?"

"Not a peep." Mercedes told her Sam hoped the judge would set bail, and she'd offered to post it so he could get out.

"Your offer is awfully generous considering what he did," Elvira said.

"I'm not sure he did anything," Mercedes said. "Other than trying to protect me from his ex."

"Did you find anything out about the Candy Cart?"

Mercedes blew air through thinned lips. "Nope. I tried ordering a 520 and ended up looking like an idiot."

"What's a 520?"

"Code word for love," Carlita said. "Instead of asking for a 420, which is code for marijuana, Mercedes told the guy she wanted some love."

"Basically, I blew it."

"It happens to the best of us," Elvira said. "So Sam is still in jail and you're not any closer to figuring out who murdered the woman?"

"We have a lead on a friend of Natalie's. His name is Peyton Price. He owns a parasailing business."

"Parasailing," Elvira repeated. "You wouldn't catch me dead in one of those contraptions. Do you have any idea what the accident statistics are?"

"No." Carlita held up a hand. "And please don't tell me, at least not until after tomorrow morning."

Elvira's eyebrows shot up. "You're going parasailing?"

"I'm still on the fence and not 100% committed."

"What time tomorrow morning?"

"At nine," Mercedes said. "On Tybee Island."

"Hang on." Elvira grabbed a clipboard off the dash and began flipping through the papers. "Awesome. When are you leaving?"

"Why?" Carlita asked.

"Because I want to watch."

"This isn't a spectator event."

"I'm not a spectator," Elvira argued. "Please? I'm wide open first thing tomorrow morning."

"We'll be leaving here around eight thirty," Mercedes said.

"Cool. I'll meet you in the alley."

Before Carlita could argue, Elvira rolled her window up and took off. "Great. Not only do I get to look forward to parasailing, but I'll also have to put up with Elvira first thing in the morning. There's not enough coffee in the county for that."

Chapter 26

"As far as you know, Sam's still in jail. You guys are going parasailing tomorrow morning and Elvira can't wait to blow up Pete's tunnel," Tony summarized.

"In a nutshell," Carlita said. "Although Pete isn't going to let Elvira blow holes in the side of his wall, even if she begs him."

"Ma also stopped by the attorney's office and got a copy of the police report."

"Oh, yeah?" Tony shoved his hands in his pockets. "What does it say?"

"We haven't had a chance to check it out." Carlita removed the envelope from her purse and set it on the table.

"I thought of something," Tony said. "What if this Peyton Price guy was the one who showed up at the pawn shop?"

"It's entirely possible," Carlita said. "Although if the investigators took a print off the gun, they would already be looking into seeing if it's a match, considering they're the ones who told Mercedes about him this morning."

"Just because someone showed up here at the pawn shop with Natalie it doesn't mean they're the killer," Mercedes pointed out.

"No," Tony agreed. "But remember, she specifically mentioned the pawn shop after you told her you didn't have the fifteen hundred bucks to pay her dealer."

"True."

"If I was the drug dealer and a customer who owed me money started insisting they had connections to a pawn shop, I would swing by and check out the inventory," Tony said. "Do you know if Peyton's Parasailing has a legit website?"

"I'm not sure." A thought popped into Carlita's head. "Maybe if we can find a photo of the guy and compare it to the pawn shop's surveillance images, you might notice similarities."

"I was thinkin' the same thing." Tony headed to the store floor to ask his employees to keep an eye on things and returned to the back.

Carlita took a seat in front of the computer and opened a new search screen. She typed in the parasailing company's name and up popped their website. She clicked on the link "about us" and studied the thumbnail photo of Peyton Price.

"It's kinda small," Mercedes said. "Does this guy look familiar?"

"No," Tony said. "See if you can make it any bigger."

Carlita clicked on the photo. Nothing happened.

"I honestly don't have a clue if this was the same guy." Tony rubbed the back of his neck. "I'm trying to remember if there was anything unusual or unique about him. Voice. Mannerisms. Appearance."

"Let's see what the police report has to say." Carlita removed the contents of the envelope and scanned the first page. "This is information we already have. Parties involved. Witness statements. A description of the crime scene."

"What does it say about the witness statements?" Mercedes asked.

Carlita handed a portion of the report to her daughter. "Basically, what we already know."

Mercedes read every single line and passed the paper to her brother. "I guess this means our parasailing investigation is all we have left."

"What about the Candy Cart?" Tony asked. "I thought you were gonna check it out."

"We tried." Mercedes told him what happened. "I'm pretty sure the guy I tried to buy from thinks I'm whacko."

"Maybe you weren't the right person for the job," her brother teased.

"Obviously not."

Carlita and her children threw out ideas, people who might be better suited to buy drugs from the food truck. Each one was quickly shot down.

Carlita drummed her fingers on the desk. "I'm running out of ideas."

"I could try it," Tony offered.

"True, but if the drug dealer is the same person who came in here with Natalie, they would easily recognize you."

"Luigi won't work," Mercedes said. "He's been all over the festival grounds."

Tony began cracking his knuckles. "I might have someone in mind."

"Who?" Mercedes asked.

"Someone you wouldn't expect. Let me work on it for a minute."

Mercedes tapped the top of her wrist. "I need to check on Sadie. I might run down to the police station to find out if they're going to spring Sam soon."

Mother and daughter parted ways in the hall, but not before Carlita made Mercedes promise to give her an update on Sam.

Back home, Carlita stopped by the restaurant where she discovered Pete's dining room manager was ill, which meant he needed to cover the dinner shift.

Restless and with time on her hands, Carlita grabbed Rambo for a leisurely stroll through the park. A freighter silently drifted along the Savannah River and she stopped to admire it, always amazed at how gracefully the large vessels navigated the river.

It reminded her of Elvira's never ending quest for treasure and the idea there might be something hidden behind the restaurant's tunnel wall. It was possible. Anything was possible. Carlita had found gems more than once. Savannah was a treasure-hunter's paradise. At least it had been for the Garlucci family.

She grudgingly admired her former neighbor's tenacity. When Elvira wanted something, she wasn't afraid to go after it. The woman could be relentless. Finding treasure was her obsession and she could only imagine how much she drove her sister nuts.

A brisk breeze blew off the water. Carlita shivered against the cold. "I should've brought a jacket, Rambo." Up ahead, she spied the new riverfront coffee cart, *Latte on the Lawn*.

"Let's grab a coffee." Carlita tugged on her pup's leash, strolling down the sidewalk until reaching the coffee cart. The tantalizing aroma of freshly brewed coffee wafted in the air.

She reached the front of the line and placed her order. A redhead with rows of braids promptly assembled her specialty coffee. "What a beautiful dog."

"This is Rambo." Carlita patted his head.

"Can he have a treat?" The young woman held up a carrot.

"He can. Give him a treat and he'll be your new best friend," she joked.

The woman exited the cart. She knelt next to Rambo and held out the carrot. He promptly gobbled up the tasty treat and licked her hand to show his appreciation. "What kind of dog is he?"

"Part doberman and part German shepherd."

"You're a fine fellow." The woman slowly stood. "I hope you enjoy your coffee."

"Thanks. It smells divine." The hot brew hit the spot, warming Carlita for the return walk home.

She briefly wondered how Mercedes was doing and if she'd found anything out about Sam.

Carlita reached for her phone and then stopped herself. Mercedes was a grown woman. Sam was a grown man. Yes, she wanted to help in whatever way she could, but she'd already told her daughter to call if she needed help.

Back home, she tidied up their spacious penthouse apartment, admiring their new painting, and then placed Mercedes' book on the bookshelf.

Rambo disappeared down the hall and she could hear the *clickety click* of his nails on the wood floor. Carlita trailed after him and followed him into what had quickly become her favorite room. The kitchen.

It was U-shaped with a large center island which included a second sink, a prep sink she found she loved to use. The spacious kitchen meant the couple had plenty of room to spread out and work side by side.

Marble countertops met white shaker cabinets. The cabinets went all the way to the ceiling. Clear glass display doors near the top added depth. Crown molding gave the room an elegant, finished look.

A custom brick arch built around the six-burner stove included a pot filler. The kitchen vibe had an Italian charm. To sum it up, it was every woman's dream, and she loved every square inch of it.

With time to kill, and suspecting Pete might be hungry when he got home, Carlita tracked down one of her snack platters. She carefully arranged generous portions of prosciutto and pepperoni and even included carved slices of salami.

She placed provolone, Asiago and gorgonzola cheeses alongside the meats, some of which she handcrafted to resemble roses. "We need olives."

Carlita grabbed a stack of ramekins. She filled one with blue cheese stuffed olives, a second with slivered almonds and a third with her homemade pesto.

Thick slices of Italian bread were next. She draped clusters of ripe green grapes in the only open spot she had left and took a step back to admire her handiwork.

Carlita turned the platter at an angle and snapped a picture of her creation, thinking she might muster up enough nerve to post it in one of the online food groups she'd joined.

Pete sent a text while she was cleaning up, asking if she wanted him to bring something home for dinner.

I have it covered, she promptly texted back and included a heart emoji.

Carlita ran to the bathroom to freshen up and by the time she got back to the kitchen, Pete was standing at the counter, admiring the spread of food. He let out a low whistle. "This is mighty fancy for an old pirate. What do they call this? A charcuterie?"

"Yep. It's called a tagliere in Italian," she said. "Pronounced tahl-yeh-reh. Mercedes has taken an interest in charcuterie after I tried my hand at it a while back. She mentioned making one for her party the other night, so I figured I would try whipping up one of my own."

"It looks tasty."

"I hope so. I had fun putting it together." Carlita opened the fridge. "What would you like to drink?"

"What are my choices?"

"Pomegranate infused water or lemonade."

"Surprise me."

"Done." Carlita filled two goblets with ice and added the flavored water. "Rough night?"

"Rough day. Rough night. How about you?" Pete let out a low groan and sank into the chair.

"The food truck was busy. I'll fill you in during dinner." Carlita grabbed some silverware. "Will this be enough food?"

"Plenty. I don't want to eat a heavy meal this late at night."

"Ditto." Carlita carried the drinks out onto the balcony while Pete followed behind with the charcuterie board and plates. "I'm a little worried about Mercedes and Sam. Last I heard, she was thinking about going down to the police station."

"She hasn't called you?" It was the way Pete asked the question that caught Carlita's attention. He seemed, for lack of a better word, distracted. "Are you all right? You seem a little preoccupied."

"A situation has come up. I'm not sure how you're going to feel about it."

Chapter 27

"Does it involve Mercedes, Sam, or the woman's death?" Carlita asked.

"It's Kris. She was out of town for work and her apartment flooded. She needs a place to stay until repairs can be made."

Kris, Pete's daughter, lived nearby and traveled extensively for her job. Which meant she wasn't home much.

"She can come stay with us," Carlita said. "We have plenty of room for her."

"With Kris's work schedule, I doubt we'll hardly ever see her."

"She can stay as long as she needs to."

Pete grimaced.

"There's more," Carlita guessed.

"I'm not sure if I've ever mentioned she has a pet."

"What kind of pet?"

"He's downstairs, in my office." Pete hurried on. "We can leave him down there if it freaks you out."

"Pete Taylor." Carlita placed her hands on her hips. "What kind of pet does Kris have?"

"I think it's best if I show you." Pete led her out of the apartment and down the back stairs to his office.

He eased the office door open and stuck his head around the corner.

Through the crack in the door, Carlita glimpsed a glowing light inside a square terrarium. From the doorway, she watched a stick rise up out of the bottom. "It's a snake."

"A ball python, to be precise," Pete said. "His name is Monty."

Carlita cautiously approached the glass enclosure, involuntarily shivering as the snake flicked his tongue at her. She blurted out the most positive thing she could think of. "He looks friendly."

"I suppose so, for a snake. Kris dropped him off earlier," Pete said. "To be frank, I'm not keen on having a snake in the apartment. If you're okay with it, we'll let him stay down here in my office."

"Monty the murderer," Gunner squawked.

"Gunner isn't sure what to think, either."

"Where did he come up with murderer?" Carlita asked. "Is there something I should know? Has Monty strangled someone?"

"No." Pete chuckled. "Remember when I said he was watching reruns of Starsky and Hutch? Gunner is continuing to add to his vocabulary."

"I'm sending you upriver for a long time," the parrot screeched. "Make a move and I'll shoot."

"Gunner seems nervous," Carlita said. "For safety's sake, I say we keep him and Rambo in the apartment and let Monty hang out here."

"Agreed." Pete gave his wife a quick hug. "Thanks for being such a good sport about it."

"You're welcome. I hope Kris will be okay with being separated from her beloved Monty."

"I think she's relieved to have a place to hang her hat. It should only be for a couple of weeks until the renovation crew can tear out the damaged drywall and replace it."

"What happened?"

"Her water heater sprung a leak and flooded her apartment." Pete told her the neighbor started noticing wet spots in the hall near her unit and called Kris, who contacted the landlord.

"She's welcome to stay as long as she needs to." Carlita warily eyed the snake, who seemed to be following her every move. "I think I'll let you take care of Monty."

"He only eats once a week. Monty is low maintenance, which is why he's the perfect pet for Kris."

"Better her than me."

Pete lifted Gunner's cage from the post and carried him upstairs to their apartment.

During dinner, Carlita filled Pete in on what she and Mercedes had found. "The bottom line is, we suspect the Candy Cart is dealing drugs but have no solid proof. Tony isn't sure the guy who came into the pawn shop at the same time as Natalie is Peyton Price. I'm still on the fence about parasailing tomorrow morning and haven't heard if Sam is still in jail."

"Tomorrow is a new day," Pete said. "Perhaps you'll get a break in the case."

"I sure hope so. This living in limbo and worrying about Sam and Mercedes is keeping me up at night." Carlita didn't add what she really wanted to say—her new concern. A slithering snake named Monty.

The mere thought of a python residing under the same roof was guaranteed to give her nightmares.

*****

The next morning, Carlita trudged to the end of the alley and found Mercedes and Elvira already waiting for her.

"You look like a zombie," Elvira said as she drew close. "With raccoon eyes."

"I didn't get much sleep last night." Carlita stifled a yawn. "Thanks for texting me to let me know Sam still hasn't been released."

"Why not?" Elvira asked. "I thought it was a done deal."

"It was never a done deal. It was a maybe deal. Basically, he's in limbo."

"At least he has three hots and a cot," Elvira quipped.

"I'm sure he would rather be anywhere else. Sadie misses him. She's been moping around the apartment and sits in front of the door, waiting for Sam. I know she wants to go home."

Carlita's heart sank. "Poor thing. She doesn't understand what's going on."

"I figured you looked tired because you're a newlywed and all. I'm sure you have a lot of action going on." Elvira made googly eyes.

"Good grief. Yes, we have a lot of action, but not in the sense you're thinking. Kris's apartment flooded. She's going to be staying with us until the repairs are made," Carlita said. "Kris and Monty."

"Who are Kris and Monty?" Elvira asked.

"Pete's daughter and her pet python."

"Eww." Elvira curled her lip. "A snake?"

"Yes. He's downstairs in Pete's office. I have to admit when I got up to go to the bathroom last night, all I could think about was him getting loose, slithering up through the vents, and sneaking into our apartment."

"I won't be coming over to your place again until the snake is gone," Elvira said.

"That's the best news I've had in days," Carlita joked.

"Why?" Elvira pouted. "Are you saying you don't enjoy my company?"

"In small doses only," Carlita said. "It also means you won't be trying to sneak inside Pete's tunnel and start chipping away at the wall, at least temporarily."

"I'm abiding by our agreement and fully intend to wait until the support posts are installed. Hopefully, the snake will be gone by then."

"You and me both." Carlita rubbed her palms together. "We should hit the road if we want to make it to Tybee Island by nine."

The women climbed into Mercedes' new compact car, the one she'd recently purchased after her mother moved out and took the Lincoln Town Car they'd shared since Vincent's death.

It had worked out in the end. The smaller car was easier for her daughter to zip around town. Because Carlita rarely drove, preferring fresh air and exercise, the black tank of a car spent most of the time parked in the driveway.

During the ride over, the women discussed the plan. It was simple. To try to figure out how close Peyton and Natalie were.

Mercedes cast her mother a mischievous side glance. "I'm proud of you, Ma."

"Why?"

"I figured you would call first thing this morning and back out."

"I thought about it."

"What made you change your mind?"

"You."

"You didn't want to let me down," Mercedes said.

"No. I wanted to prove a point. You can do anything you set your mind to. Overcoming obstacles. Facing your fears. Yeah, I'm terrified, but I also figured if it was my time to go, it's my time to go."

"The only place I plan on going is up." Mercedes jabbed her finger skyward. "The view is going to be incredible."

"I'm sure it will."

Elvira sat in the backseat, quietly listening to the conversation.

Carlita flipped the visor down and stared at her in the mirror. "Why are you so quiet?"

"I was thinking."

"About what?"

"Zulilly."

Elvira's daughter had gotten into trouble some time back. Which was an understatement. The woman had murdered her father's girlfriend, insisting she'd done him a favor. Showing signs of mental illness, Zulilly had been admitted to an area prison's mental health ward.

"How is she?" Carlita asked softly.

"The same. Still in the mental hospital. Still believing she did Gremlin, my ex, a favor by killing Kim."

"I'm sorry to hear that."

"I visit about once a month. She knows who I am, knows her father and she seems...content." Elvira's eyes shined with unshed tears. "I wish things had turned out differently for Zu."

"Me too," Carlita said. "Life doesn't always give us a fair shake."

"Nope."

"We're here." Mercedes pulled into the parking lot and into an empty spot. "It looks like the crew is already prepping for our adventure."

Elvira unbuckled and tapped Carlita on the shoulder. "Your face is white as a ghost. Are you sure you're going to do this?"

"No. Yes." Carlita reached for the door handle. "Let's get this over with before I change my mind."

Chapter 28

Carlita was almost certain the man who greeted them near the boat dock was the same one she and Mercedes had seen on Peyton Price's parasailing website. Her suspicions were confirmed when he introduced himself.

"Good morning. I'm Peyton Price, the owner of Peyton's Parasailing."

Mercedes held out her hand. "I'm Mercedes, the one who called you yesterday."

"It's nice to meet you." Peyton grasped Mercedes' hand, holding it a little longer than was necessary, and the smile never left his face as he leaned in. "You look familiar. Have we met before?"

"I...don't think so." Mercedes hurriedly introduced her mother. "This is Carlita Taylor, my mom."

"We have room for three to parasail." Peyton gave Elvira the once over. "Will you be joining these lovely ladies?"

"No way. I'm here purely for entertainment purposes," Elvira said. "I'll keep both feet firmly planted on terra firma."

"You can ride along in the boat. We're not booked out today, if you're interested in riding along."

Elvira eyed the boat and workers who were tinkering with something near the back. "Nah. I figure there will be a lot of screaming going on. I kind of like my hearing as it is. Thanks for the offer, though."

"You've already prepaid. All we need now is for you both to sign off on a few forms and we'll be on our way." Peyton grabbed a clipboard from the stand and passed it to Carlita.

"What is this?"

"Release of liability," he said.

"Meaning if we're injured, we die, end up paralyzed, or any sort of mishap occurs, we can't sue you or your company," Carlita summarized.

"In a nutshell."

"And if we don't sign?"

"If you don't sign, you don't sail," he joked.

"C'mon, Ma." Mercedes playfully nudged her mother's arm. "Nothing will happen."

"How long have you been in business?" Carlita asked.

"Five years."

"Any accidents or incidents of significance?"

"One. A young passenger thought it would be fun to cut the rope."

Carlita's jaw dropped. "Cut the rope?"

"He almost succeeded. Thankfully, one of our watchers saw what he was doing, and we brought him in."

"What a dumb thing to do," Mercedes said.

"He ended up paying for damaging the equipment." Peyton rubbed his palms together. "By the time you pop back down, you're going to want to book your next parasailing adventure," he predicted.

"I wouldn't hold my breath," Carlita muttered as she signed off.

"Let's get to it." Mercedes quickly signed and began making her way toward the dock.

Her mother grabbed her arm and pulled her back. "Remember why we're here," she whispered in Mercedes' ear.

"Right." She whispered back. "To find out how close Peyton and Natalie were."

"Bon voyage." Elvira removed a pair of binoculars from her backpack and draped them around her neck. "I can't believe you're going to do this."

"You and me both." Carlita reluctantly trailed behind her daughter and Peyton. She reached the dock and lingered. She still had time to change her mind.

But then she noticed the look on Mercedes' face. It was the first genuine smile she'd seen in days—long before Natalie showed up and she and Sam broke up.

She cast a wistful glance toward Elvira, who was standing near the water's edge. She crossed her fingers, wishing her luck. And at that moment, Carlita would've paid a hundred bucks to trade places with her. A hundred in cold hard cash.

Sucking in a breath, Carlita boarded the small boat, sealing her fate.

Despite trying to pay attention to the instructions while they made their way out into the water, Carlita's mind wandered. *What if the winds were too high? What if the boat had engine trouble? The water seemed a little choppy. Would it be a rough ride?*

The boat slowed. She numbed herself to the process, allowing Peyton and his crew to help her with her life jacket. They hooked both their jackets to the harnesses before attaching them to the rope which would lift them up in the air. All the while, the only thing Carlita could think was, *have I lost my mind?*

It seemed like only seconds before mother and daughter were being guided to the platform.

Peyton motioned to Carlita. "You sit on this side. Mercedes will sit next to you."

"S-sit down?" she stammered.

"Yes. You sit down," he patiently explained. "As soon as you're in position, you'll gradually glide up into the air."

"It's like floating," Mercedes said. "Peyton already explained the entire process."

"I...was thinking about other stuff." *Falling. Hitting the water. The rope breaking.*

"We'll be fine." Mercedes grasped the straps, the smile never leaving her face.

Meanwhile, Carlita's heart hammered loudly in her chest. She tried swallowing, but her mouth was so dry, she started to choke. Out of the corner of her eye, she glimpsed Elvira still standing on the shoreline, binoculars zeroed in on them.

Carlita could've sworn the woman was smiling. Smiling as widely as Mercedes, but for entirely different reasons.

In tandem, the women lifted off, gradually going higher and higher until they were far above the water. Far from the boat, from shore, from help.

Stop, Carlita scolded. *You're up here. You might as well enjoy the view.* She forced herself to look around, to enjoy the beauty of Tybee Island, the open water, the clear blue skies.

It was hard to tell how long she and Mercedes were parasailing. It seemed like only a minute before they started descending. And it was smooth, much smoother than Carlita envisioned.

They dipped down, their feet lightly brushing the water before landing upright on the platform.

Peyton stood waiting for them. "Well?"

"It was amazing," Mercedes gushed. "Like floating and flying. It was peaceful and beautiful."

"And what about you, Mom?" Peyton began unstrapping her harness.

"I'm still in one piece. I didn't pass out, and the view was incredible."

"Incredible enough for you to want to go parasailing again?" he asked.

"Not on your life. This was a one and done." Carlita held out her still trembling hand. "I'm glad I did it. Once."

Mercedes rummaged around in her bag and pulled out her cell phone. "Do you mind if I get a picture of you, me and my mom?"

"Of course not." Peyton squeezed in, cozily leaning toward Mercedes with Carlita on her other side. She snapped a selfie and then checked to see how it turned out. "Perfect. Thank you for holding our hands and helping us enjoy our parasailing adventure."

"You're welcome." Peyton lowered his eyelids. "Maybe you and I can grab a drink sometime."

The man had given Carlita the perfect opening. Actually, he'd dropped it in her lap. "You live nearby?"

"In Savannah."

"Us too," Carlita said. "I'm only a stone's throw away from the Savannah River."

"Ma is married to the owner of the Parrot House Restaurant."

"No kidding." Peyton arched a brow. "I love that place. I heard the owner, which would be your husband, is part pirate."

"He is," Carlita said. "Pete also owns the pirate ship, The Flying Gunner."

"Cool. I've been meaning to check it out. It looks like fun."

"They host a lot of themed cruises." Carlita rattled off a few of the more popular ones. "Maybe you could bring your girlfriend or a friend."

"No girlfriend. All my female friends are strictly platonic." Peyton stashed the harness gear in the bins. "Do you ever listen to live music downtown?"

"Yeah," Mercedes said. "Me and my friends hang out at The Thirsty Crow. Have you heard of Cool Bones and the Jazz Boys?"

"I sure have. They're one of the better bands. You know them?" Peyton asked.

"Ma owns some rental units. Cool Bones is a tenant," Mercedes explained.

"They're playing downtown this weekend. Maybe you and I could meet up and hang out," Peyton said.

"I would except I've curtailed some of my nighttime activities," Mercedes said. "A woman was murdered a couple of days ago. As far as I know, her killer still hasn't been caught."

"Natalie Lameron." Peyton's expression sobered. "She was a friend of mine."

Mercedes pressed a hand to her chest. "Oh my gosh. I am so sorry."

"She was in town visiting and kind of down on her luck. I loaned her my couch so she would have a place to crash." Peyton fiddled with the equipment, his voice cracking. "When she didn't come back the other night..."

Carlita touched his arm. "You must have been close."

"We were. I don't want to go into detail, but Natalie was...she made some bad decisions."

"Do you have any idea who might have killed her, or do you think it was random?" Mercedes asked.

"She knew her killer." Peyton's expression morphed from one of sorrow to anger. "Natalie got mixed up in drugs. She owed her dealer some money and was trying to work out a way to pay him. He was threatening her. Natalie never would name names, so I have no idea who it was."

"I'm sure you contacted the police to let them know," Carlita said.

"I told them everything. It could've been her ex, I suppose."

"Her ex?"

"He lives in the area. They broke up a while ago. Like years ago. Natalie was hoping to reconcile."

Mercedes dug her fingernails into the palm of her hand, on the fence about asking the question she was dying to know. "Did it seem like they were going to make it work out?"

"No. He was dating someone else. Natalie said she saw the woman. She wasn't very pretty, was whiny, and she had no idea what he saw in her."

Carlita could see her daughter fighting the urge to clap back with a snappy reply and nudged her with her toe. "Or it could be Natalie was desperate to get back together. The ex wasn't interested, so she started picking the woman apart to make herself feel better."

Peyton thought about it. "Yeah. Natalie could be judgmental. She was also beautiful...gorgeous enough to work as a model. She was a big dose of sunshine with a pinch of hurricane."

Carlita purposely changed the subject, asking Peyton general questions. How long he'd lived in Savannah. If he had other interests besides parasailing.

They arrived back at the dock without incident. Carlita tipped the boat crew, thanking them for a memorable adventure.

Elvira waited for them to reach the parking lot and hurried over. "I got some great pictures. I bet you could see almost all of Tybee Island. Did you feel like throwing up?"

"It was touch and go for a minute," Carlita said. "I have to say, it was smooth sailing, literally. And beautiful. The sky, the water, Tybee Island. It definitely gave me a different perspective."

"So, you would do it again?"

"Not a chance."

"I would," Mercedes said. "Maybe Autumn and I will go next time."

"She can't," Carlita reminded her. "Her doctor told her she couldn't do those kinds of activities, at least for now."

"Crud. You're right."

Elvira trailed behind them, following them back to Mercedes' car. "Were you able to find anything out about Natalie?"

"Yeah. She'd been staying with Peyton Price. He corroborated the fact the woman was on drugs and owed her drug dealer money."

"Did he have any idea who it was?"

"No. Peyton claims she wouldn't name names," Carlita said. "I don't think he killed her. Why would he?"

"Unless he was in love with her, they argued and he snapped," Mercedes said.

"Again, it would be a dumb move on his part, considering she'd made numerous recent calls to him," Carlita pointed out.

"True. Still." Mercedes started the car and shifted into drive. "He was giving me a weird vibe."

"Because he's attracted to you." Carlita made googly eyes.

"Even though I'm ugly."

"Natalie only said that because she was jealous."

"It doesn't matter. Even if Sam and I call it quits for good, Peyton isn't my type." Mercedes pulled onto the road leading back to the mainland. "I had hoped we were finally getting somewhere. Instead, it feels like we took three steps forward and two steps back."

Chapter 29

"Tony sent a text asking us to swing by the pawn shop on our way home. He has an idea."

"We need all the help we can get," Mercedes said.

"If your hunch is right about the Candy Cart dealing drugs and Natalie owed them money, you're running out of time," Elvira pointed out.

"Because today is the last day of the art festival." Carlita tugged on her seatbelt.

"I'm almost positive the person in line before me yesterday was buying drugs and the guy behind the counter stuck it in a brown bag for him," Mercedes said.

"I have some recording devices I use for my investigative services business. If you figure out a way to get audio of them selling drugs, you can turn it over to the cops."

"It still doesn't link Natalie to them," Carlita said.

"One step at a time, Ma. The first is to prove they're dealing drugs. Natalie was over there talking to those people. Somehow they're linked. I'm sure of it."

They reached the alley's parking lot. All three climbed out and traipsed to the pawn shop's rear entrance.

Hanging out in the back were Steve White, Dernice, and a man who looked vaguely familiar. Except for his gray hair and cheesy moustache, along with a mole, a large one on the bottom of his chin.

"Hello." Carlita curiously eyed the stranger.

"Hello, Mrs. GT," Steve said. "I heard you went parasailing."

"Yes. It was exciting, but never again."

"Were you able to find anything out?"

"I don't think Peyton Price was involved in Natalie's death." Carlita listed the reasons. "He would be dumb to kill her, considering she was sleeping on his couch."

"He also seemed pretty broken up about it." Mercedes tweaked the stranger's moustache.

Horrified, Carlita pushed her away. "Mercedes Garlucci. What on earth are you doing?"

"That's what I thought."

The mustached stranger grinned. "Busted."

"What is going on?"

Elvira circled the guy, a look of pride on her face. "I get it now. Dernice did this."

"Did what?"

"It's me, Ma." The stranger leaned in. "Tony."

"You're wearing a disguise."

357

"I think I did a pretty good job, if I do say so myself." Dernice playfully patted herself on the back. "It was Luigi's idea."

"You learned from the best," Elvira boasted. "You gotta watch the glue, though. It'll give you a rash if you leave it on your skin for too long."

"It's already starting to itch."

"You're gonna try to buy drugs from the Candy Cart," Carlita guessed.

"Yep. The sooner the better."

"I ran into Tony. He told me Mercedes wasn't having any luck, so I figured I would volunteer to help," Steve said. "I know plenty about the lingo, how to make a purchase, complete a transaction."

"I have equipment you can borrow." Elvira turned to go. Dernice stopped her. "I'm one step ahead of you." She grabbed a black watch off the counter and dangled it in front of them.

Elvira made an unhappy noise, attempting to snatch the watch from her sister's hand. "What are you doing with my watch?"

Dernice, anticipating her move, scooted out of snatching range. "We're loaning it to Tony and Steve."

"I was gonna give them a pocket recorder."

"Which isn't nearly as effective as this recording watch," her sister pointed out.

"I haven't had time to test it," Elvira argued. "It might not work."

"C'mon. You and I both know this works great to record conversations. Don't be so stingy."

"It cost me a pretty penny."

"We'll be careful with it."

Elvira frowned as her sister handed the watch to Tony, who promptly strapped it on his wrist. "Thanks, Dernice."

"This baby does it all. It has one-touch recording and can record voices up to 50 feet away." Dernice showed Tony how it worked. "You won't have any problem."

"You break it, you buy it," Elvira grumbled.

Steve nudged Tony. "Let's head out before Elvira changes her mind."

"Hang on." Dernice handed him a cable. "This connects to any computer. You'll need it to transfer data."

"Meaning if we make a successful transaction, we can take it down to the police station," Tony said.

"Yes."

"Again, we still need to connect the dots," Carlita warned. "Yes, they could be drug dealers, but did they sell drugs to Natalie and, if so, who killed her?"

"All we can do is try," Steve said. "This shouldn't take long."

Carlita watched her son and Steve slip out the back door. Would it work? Would they be able to buy the goods? And even if they did, how could they link Natalie and the Candy Cart? There was no smoking gun, no solid proof.

She crossed her fingers, praying they would finally get a break, some valuable piece of information.

*****

Tony casually sauntered over to the Candy Cart, waiting patiently behind a group of teens. The guy at the counter disappeared. He returned moments later with a paper bag. They completed their transaction, and Tony stepped forward. "Hey, man. I got a friend who said you got some 420 bags. I was hoping to score some stuff."

The man leaned an elbow on the counter. "Who is your friend?"

Tony was expecting this, waiting for this question. Thankfully, Steve, who was lingering nearby, had given him the name of a tattoo customer. A customer who was also a heavy pot smoker. "Kean. You know him?"

His expression relaxed. He extended his hand. "Kean is a cool dude. My friends call me Pooler."

"And I'm Tony."

"Hey, Tony. What can I get you?"

"What do you have?"

"Deluxe bags, premium bags or economy bags, depending on your budget," Pooler said.

"I'll take a premium bag." Tony removed a tidy stack of bills from his pocket, counted out the amount, and set them on the counter.

Pooler went to the back. He returned moments later, paper bag in hand. They completed the transaction and Tony walked away, his bag of pot in hand.

Steve fell into step. "You scored some stuff."

"Thanks to you. He wasn't going to sell until I mentioned Kean's name."

"I figured as much. Did you see the guy's tattoo?"

"He said his name was Pooler. I noticed the tattoo. Is it one of your designs?"

"Not mine, but it matches the one Natalie Lameron had when she showed up at my tattoo shop the other day."

Tony stopped in his tracks. "No kidding. The Candy Cart drug dealer and Natalie had matching tattoos?"

"Yep. One hundred percent. You mentioned you had a fingerprint from the guy who was admiring a pawn shop gun, the one who stopped in at the same time as Natalie." Steve hustled to keep up with Tony's quick steps.

"The cops have it too. If they can match Pooler's fingerprints to the one on the knife, they have their guy," Tony said. "Let's swing by the pawn shop to listen to the recording."

On their way, Tony texted his mother to let her know he and Steve were heading back.

Dernice, Elvira, Carlita and Mercedes were still inside when the men returned.

Taking turns, they filled them in on what they'd discovered. The group gathered around the computer while Elvira and Dernice transferred the taped conversation.

All were quiet as they listened to the transaction between Pooler and Tony.

Steve waited until the recording ended. "This guy, Pooler, has the same tattoo as Natalie did. Same arm. Same location. Same pattern. They even used the same color ink."

"Pooler." Mercedes briefly closed her eyes. "I've heard the name. I'm almost positive Natalie said the name Pooler."

"A lot was going on that night," Carlita said.

Mercedes pressed her fingertips to her forehead. "It was when she first showed up. Natalie said something about being sure we had stuff inside the pawn shop Pooler would be interested in."

Carlita could feel the blood drain from her face. She pulled her cell phone from her pocket and tapped the screen. "No way. Pooler, Georgia. The Candy Cart's address is 1512 County Line Road, Pooler, Georgia. It's right there on their food truck permit."

"Natalie's Pooler is the Candy Cart drug dealer. I would bet my life his fingerprint will match the one on the knife," Mercedes said. "We might not have to spring Sam from jail after all."

"Send me a copy, Ma."

Carlita forwarded the picture to her son. "All the cops have to do now is connect the dots."

Elvira cleared her throat.

"What is it?" Carlita asked.

"The watch."

"We need the audio," Mercedes said. "It's potential evidence."

"May I?" Elvira motioned to the computer.

Tony stepped aside.

She tapped the keys. "I texted it to Carlita."

Carlita's cell phone chimed. "Got it. I'm sending a copy to Tony."

Tony handed the watch to her. "Thanks for the loan."

"You're welcome. I'm glad I could be of assistance," she said.

"I guess I don't need this anymore." Tony peeled off the fake moustache and removed the wig. He handed both to Dernice. "Thanks for the disguise."

"You met Pooler. Do you recognize him from being here in the pawn shop with Natalie?" Mercedes asked.

Tony thought about it. "No. Whoever it was intentionally avoided looking directly at the cameras. I'm ready to head down to the station."

Mercedes took a step toward the door. "Do you mind if I tag along? If we're lucky, we can track down Detective Polivich, show him what we have, and be there when they let Sam out of jail."

"Sam's lucky to have you," Dernice said. "I don't know too many women who would stand by their man's side after going through something like this."

Elvira waved dismissively. "This is nothing for the Garlucci family. They're a magnet for difficult situations."

"I would say the same about you, Elvira Cobb," Carlita said. "Although most of your situations are self-inflicted."

Tony waved his phone in the air. "Let's get this show on the road and see if we can get Sam out of jail."

Chapter 30

Beep...beep...beep.

Carlita jumped out of the way, narrowly missing being sideswiped by a big box truck backing into the Parrot House Restaurant's parking lot. "Are you expecting a delivery?"

"No." Pete shook his head. "My food truck delivery came in yesterday."

The truck shuddered to a stop. The driver's side door flew open. Elvira hopped out. "It's a beautiful morning."

"What is this?" Carlita motioned to the truck.

"I rented a truck."

"Why? And why did you bring it here?"

"Because I couldn't fit all my equipment in the work van." Elvira flipped the latch and lifted the rolling door.

"Blimey," Pete gasped. "It's full of tools."

"Yep." Elvira proudly patted the side. "Everything we could possibly need to tear into your basement wall."

"I think this might be a bit premature," Carlita warned.

"Why? Wempley is here, installing the support posts."

"Yes, he is," Pete said. "He hasn't given us the green light to chip away at my tunnel wall."

"Merely a formality." Elvira dusted her hands. "It's in the bag. How long has he been here?"

"A couple of hours," Pete said. "He should be finishing soon."

"I'll go check on him." She started to grab a toolbox. Carlita stopped her. "I think you should leave everything here until they're done. You'll only be in their way."

"It's gonna take several trips." Elvira grabbed a black bag. "At least let me bring this."

Carlita and Pete exchanged a glance.

"I think you're jumping the gun. You unload, you get to lug it around."

They reached the doorway, and Elvira hesitated.

"Now what?" Carlita asked.

"Do you still have company?"

"Company?" she echoed.

"Pete's daughter and Monty the python."

"Kris's snake," Pete said. "Monty is in my office. At least he was last time I checked."

"Is his enclosure secure?" Elvira rubbed the sides of her arms, a look of trepidation on her face. "I have this fear of reptiles. Venomous snakes in particular."

"Monty is a ball python. He's non-venomous."

"What about strangulation?"

"He's too small to strangle a person."

"Good to know." Elvira swallowed hard. "You're sure he's secured away?"

"Yes."

"Okay. Because I'm trusting you to be up front about this."

"No one is twisting your arm. Either stay here or follow me. You decide." Pete led the way into the back of the restaurant. They reached the stairs accessing the lower level and tunnel.

All the while, Elvira rambled on about how they would start by removing several smaller bricks in the center of the tunnel corridor. "I figure we should try dead center. See what's up and move right or left from there."

The trio arrived to find Wempley and his crew installing the third and final post.

"This is it." Elvira licked her lips, barely able to contain her excitement. "I have been waiting for this day forever."

"More like waiting for about a week." Carlita rolled her eyes.

"I've been on the hunt for treasure since I moved to Walton Square. This is the culmination of all my hard work."

"I have to say you never gave up," Pete said. "I admire your tenacity."

"And it's all going to pay off. In spades. Once word gets out, we'll be local celebrities. I look at this as a double bonus."

"How so?" Carlita asked.

"Not only will Pete and I be household names, but our businesses will too." Elvira unzipped the sides of the flat canvas bag she brought with her and pulled out a large posterboard sign. In bold green neon letters was *EC Investigative Services*.

She flipped it over to the reverse side, *EC Security Services*. "You can't miss this, eh?"

"Not at all." Carlita shaded her eyes. "The letters are burning my retinas."

"Very funny." Elvira set the sign aside. "It looks like they're almost done."

"I have to say, Mr. Wempley doesn't mess around," Pete said.

"Because I was bugging him every single day." Elvira took a step back, motioning Pete and Carlita away from the workers. "How are Mercedes and Sam doing?"

Carlita tipped her hand back and forth. "It's going to take time for Mercedes to build back a level of trust. She's trying, but she's also being cautious."

"I don't blame her," Elvira said. "Talk about determination. She was a woman on a mission, determined to figure out who killed Natalie."

"Yes, she was." Carlita tapped the side of her forehead. "Mercedes is good at putting the pieces together. She suspected from the get-go the Candy Cart was involved in Natalie's death."

Elvira puffed out her chest. "Let's not forget I pointed you in the right direction by telling you candy was slang for drugs *and* I loaned you the recording device, proving they were dealing drugs."

"Reluctantly loaned the recording watch," Carlita reminded her. "Mercedes remembered seeing Natalie talking with one of the employees the first day she showed up at our food truck. Sam knew his ex was in trouble, but I don't think he realized how deep until she became desperate and tried to get to Mercedes."

"Mercedes is bummed that she missed an important clue when Natalie mentioned the name Pooler. We knew Edward Stockton, the owner of the Candy Cart, listed a Pooler, Georgia address, but never put two and two together."

"She needs to cut herself some slack," Elvira said. "Judging by how the woman was acting on my surveillance cameras, it would be hard to concentrate on what she was saying. I would be more focused on making sure she didn't make it up the fire escape and onto my balcony."

Pete tapped his wife's shoulder. "Don't forget the pawn shop's surveillance video showing Natalie inside the shop with Pooler."

"Although it wasn't a clear shot of him inside the store," Carlita reminded them. "Looking back, she brought her drug dealer, who was also her ex-boyfriend, right to our front door."

"I have to say, if not for Steve and Tony successfully buying a bag and noticing Pooler's tattoo, we might never have been able to link them. He and Natalie had matching recovery tattoos," Pete said.

"Plenty of clues were pointing to Travis 'Pooler' Stockton," Elvira said. "I heard from my contact at the police station, when Pooler was brought in for questioning, he refused to take a DNA test."

"So the cops had to get a warrant," Carlita guessed. "I thought for sure they would have a print from the knife and could match it to the fingerprints on the gun Pooler was handling inside our pawn shop."

"It's a good thing Pooler's DNA sample matched DNA from the crime scene," Elvira said. "He won't be back on the streets selling drugs for a very long time."

Carlita shifted her feet. "I feel sorry for Mr. Stockton, Pooler's dad. He had no idea his son was dealing drugs. He thought he was selling candy and sweets."

Stuart Wempley made his way over. "My guys are wrapping up here. We're almost done."

Elvira whooped loudly. "I'm so excited, I can hardly stand still. I have my tools out in the van. All you have to do is give me the word."

"Unfortunately, I have a slight bit of bad news," the engineer said.

"Bad news?" Elvira scowled.

"Follow me."

The trio followed him over to the center support post. "I believe at one time, this tunnel floor was level. Over the years, and based on its proximity to the river, it settled. Unfortunately, it settled in all the wrong places."

"Meaning?" Pete prompted.

"This center support is the most important one. The structure, meaning your restaurant's floor, is now secure, but I would like to give it a little time to make sure the support post doesn't shift."

"Because if the post shifts, it means there's a chance my floor shifts," Pete said.

"Correct." Wempley went into a long drawn out explanation again about weight distribution, load bearing requirements, the age of the structure.

Finally, Elvira cut him off. "Stop with the technical mumbo jumbo. When can we start with some exploratory wall removal?"

"It won't be for at least two weeks," the engineer said.

"Two weeks?" Elvira gasped. "You're killing me here. I thought installing posts was going to ensure we could begin working."

"It will...soon, but not today. The bottom line is I can't guarantee the integrity of your structure until I'm able to ensure it remains secure."

"We'll wait," Pete said.

Elvira placed her hands on the sides of her head, a pained expression on her face. "I can't believe this. Let's get a second opinion."

"Stop!" Pete cut her off. "We've waited this long. We can wait a little longer."

"So close and yet so far." Elvira snatched up her bag and stormed off, muttering under her breath about incompetence and how life wasn't fair.

Pete extended his hand, and Wempley shook it. "Thank you for being cautious. I appreciate your thoroughness and not rushing to push this project to a conclusion."

"You're welcome." The engineer pressed on the bridge of his glasses. "Unfortunately, knowing Elvira, I think this might be a very long couple of weeks for all of us."

"Without a doubt," Carlita chuckled. "It will most definitely be a long couple of weeks."

The end.

Dear Reader,

I hope you enjoyed reading, "Secrets in Savannah." Would you please take a moment to leave a review? It would mean so much. Thank you! -Hope Callaghan

The Series Continues!

Read the next book in the series,
"Shakedown in Savannah"

Join the Fun

Get Updates On New Releases, FREE and
Discounted eBooks, Giveaways, & More!

hopecallaghan.com

Read More by Hope

Made in Savannah Cozy Mystery Series

After the mysterious death of her mafia "made man" husband, Carlita Garlucci makes a shocking discovery. Follow the Garlucci family saga as Carlita and her daughter try to escape their NY mob ties and make a fresh start in Savannah, Georgia. They soon realize you can run but can't hide from your past.

Easton Island Mystery Series

Easton Island is the continuing saga of one woman's journey from incredible loss to finding a past she knew nothing about, including a family who both embraces and fears her and a charming island that draws her in. This inspirational women's fiction series is for lovers of family sagas, friendship, mysteries, and clean romance.

Cruise Director Millie Mystery Series

Cruise Director Millie Mystery Series is the new spin-off series from the wildly popular Millie's Cruise Ship Cozy Mysteries.

Millie's Cruise Ship Cozy Mystery Series

Hoping for a fresh start after her recent divorce, sixty something Millie Sanders, lands her dream job as the assistant cruise director onboard the "Siren of the Seas." Too bad no one told her murder is on the itinerary.

Lack of Luxury Series (Liz and the Garden Girls)

Green Acres meets the Golden Girls in this brand new cozy mystery spin-off series featuring Liz and the Garden Girls!

Garden Girls Cozy Mystery Series

A lonely widow finds new purpose for her life when she and her senior friends help solve a murder in their small Midwestern town.

Garden Girls - The Golden Years

The brand new spin-off series of the Garden Girls Mystery series! You'll enjoy the same fun-loving characters as they solve mysteries in the cozy town of Belhaven. Each book will focus on one of the Garden Girls as they enter their "golden years."

Divine Cozy Mystery Series

After relocating to the tiny town of Divine, Kansas, strange and mysterious things begin to happen to businesswoman, Jo Pepperdine and those around her.

Samantha Rite Mystery Series

Heartbroken after her recent divorce, a single mother is persuaded to book a cruise and soon finds herself caught in the middle of a deadly adventure. Will she make it out alive?

Sweet Southern Sleuths Short Stories Series

Twin sisters with completely opposite personalities become amateur sleuths when a dead body is discovered in their recently inherited home in Misery, Mississippi.

Meet Hope Callaghan

Hope Callaghan is an American mystery author who loves to write clean, fun-filled women's fiction mysteries with a touch of faith and romance. She is the author of more than 100 novels in ten different series.

Born and raised in a small town in West Michigan, she now lives in Florida with her husband. She is the proud mother of 3 wonderful children.

When she's not doing the thing she loves best - writing mysteries - she enjoys cooking, traveling and reading books.

Get a free cozy mystery book, new release alerts, and giveaways at <u>hopecallaghan.com</u>

Dark Chocolate Chip Peanut Butter Pie Recipe

Ingredients:

Crust:

3/4 cup graham cracker crumbs

1/4 cup granulated sugar

4 tablespoons melted butter

Filling:

1 1/2 cups heavy cream

8 ounces cream cheese, softened

3/4 cup granulated sugar

1 cup creamy peanut butter

1 tablespoon vanilla extract

1 cup mini dark chocolate chips

Directions:

To assemble crust:

-In bottom of glass pie plate, blend graham cracker crumbs, sugar and melted butter.

-Press evenly along bottom and sides of the pie plate.

-Chill in freezer.

To make pie filling:

-Using mixer, whip heavy cream until peaks form. Set aside.

-In a large bowl, beat cream cheese until smooth.

-Add sugar, peanut butter, and vanilla. Blend well.

-Fold in the whipped cream and mini dark chocolate chips until evenly distributed.

-Remove chilled crust from fridge.

-Pour filling into the crust, distributing evenly.

-Return to freezer and chill until firm. *

-Just before serving, thaw pie (est. 20 minutes).

*If you want a softer pie, you can put it in the fridge to chill.

Made in the USA
Columbia, SC
26 March 2024